TWELVE DOGS OF CHRISTMAS

A FESTIVE HOLIDAY TALE

MELISSA HILL

CONTENTS

TWELVE DOGS OF CHRISTMAS

CHRISTMAS BENEATH THE STARS

TWELVE DOGS OF CHRISTMAS

A FESTIVE HOLIDAY TAIL

CHAPTER 1

*T*he curtains were wide open when Lucy Adams woke up. She must have forgotten to close them the night before, and now she was glad for that.

Snow outlined the windowsill like a frame, and the blanketed San Juan Mountains - the sun just peeking above its summit - was the picture.

It was a beautiful sight to wake up to.

She sighed happily. Small-town life was very different to what it had been like in Denver, but she should have known the city wasn't for her.

Lucy was a Whitedale native, born and bred.

Once upon a time, she thought that time in the big city would help her shyness, and allow her to live out her grandmother's dream of her becoming a success.

Gran had been so sure that Lucy becoming an investigative journalist and seeing her name on the by-line of a story would have spurred her on to even greater things, but it didn't.

Because she never got any further than being a fact-checker.

Lucy was cripplingly shy; always had been. When she was a child her mother tried everything to help bring her out of her shell, but it was no use.

Her timidity and innate reserve around people made it difficult for her to even broach the subject of an article to her boss.

In the end, she realized that no matter how hard she tried, she'd never be as happy in Denver as she would be back home.

So home she came.

Now, she swung her legs from beneath the sheets and did a few quick stretches to loosen herself up for the day ahead. Then quickly made her bed; the wrinkled sheets and pillow depressed on only one side.

Her apartment was the best she could afford; a small upper-level two-bed on Maypole Avenue, close to all the parks and trails.

When she started renting it a couple of years ago, she'd sort of hoped that by now she'd have someone to share it with, but no such luck.

Lucy didn't know why, but she seemed to have been born without the romance gene too.

She knew she wasn't bad-looking, with her shoulder-length caramel-coloured hair and fair skin. Her smile was big and warm, but the problem likely was that she didn't really smile around people.

Animals yes; humans not so much.

People made her nervous, which was why having a dog-walking business was a plus. Lucy spent her days surrounded by those who understood her without judgment.

Lucy was very proud of her business, 12 Dogs Walking Service. It was the premier dog-walking outfit in town, and she had dreams of making it even better.

Once she had enough money saved and found the right location, she fully intended to add other services, like doggie daycare and pet pampering.

She envisioned her little business as one day being the best animal care centre in the county, if not the state.

But hey, one day at a time.

THE WOODEN FLOORS were cool beneath her feet as Lucy left her bedroom and walked into the kitchen.

She fixed herself a bowl of cereal and a cup of coffee while waiting for her computer to wake.

She loved her trusty old-model Dell PC, but Betsy was on her last legs. It used to take less than a minute for it to boot up, now it was more like seven.

Lucy hummed the lyrics to *Must Have Been the Mistletoe* as she got out her apple cinnamon granola and almond milk. She did her best to eat well, and in Whitedale that was made easier by the popularity of the farm-to-table movement.

Then she settled at her two-seater dining table by the small window overlooking the square.

The town was slowly coming to life - in a few hours, cars and people would be bustling along the streets, but for the moment it was just store owners looking for an early start, and a few joggers out for a morning run.

When the PC was fully loaded, the home screen flickered to life, and a picture of a golden-haired cocker spaniel greeted Lucy, making her smile immediately.

"So let's see what's going on today..." she mumbled as she opened her emails; a couple of subscription updates to animal magazines and journals, and a few more notifying her of pet trade shows in the area.

Then requests from her clients.

Bob St. John wanted Blunders walked on Thursday. He was a new client and Blunders, a three-year-old dachshund, was sorely in need of Lucy's services.

Bob, loving owner that he was, had been won over by Blunder's pleading looks, and now the dog was carrying a little too much weight. The extra pounds for a larger breed might've been easier to handle, but the dachshund's long body made it more easily prone to herniated discs.

The sooner Blunders got the exercise in, and if Bob stuck to the diet the vet had recommended, Lucy was sure that the little dog would be fine in no time.

"Dear Bob ..." she intoned out loud, as she began to type a response confirming the date and time, and set an alert reminder for herself on her phone.

Martha Bigsby wanted Charlie walked every day that week. Charlie was a six-year-old Airedale Terrier. His coat was perfect and thankfully so was his health. He was Martha's prize-winning pooch and she loved him dearly.

Lucy loved owners who shared her appreciation for their animals. Charlie had a big show coming up before the holidays, and she wanted to be sure he was ready for it.

Dear Martha. I confirm that I'll pick up Charlie at seven each morning this week. We can return to our normal nine o'clock slot once you're back from Bakersfield.

She spent the next twenty minutes replying to her work emails before checking her personal ones, though was finished with those in less than one.

Lucy's life consisted mostly of work, and very little of the social aspects that most other people found entertaining. Socialising just wasn't her thing really.

She'd always been happier around animals than people. They, especially dogs, were easy to understand and predictable for the most part.

People weren't, and that was a difficulty for Lucy. She liked what she could rely on and she'd been disappointed far too many times by people.

Never by her furry friends.

Her phone rang then and she checked the caller display. It was Eustacia, her neighbour on the floor below; a woman who believed it was her job to marry off every singleton in their building.

"Lucy? Are you there? Of course, you're there. You're screening my calls aren't you?" Eustacia's Brooklyn accent pierced her ears.

Her new neighbour, who had moved from New York

four months ago, was convinced she knew what was best for Lucy, and that she'd find her the 'perfect guy'.

"Trust me. I know all about these things. At home, they used to call me the matchmaker. I can set up anyone with anyone. You leave it to me. A young girl like you shouldn't be all alone every night. It's ain't natural."

Lucy would've appreciated the help if it weren't for the fact that Eustacia had terrible taste in men.

"Mrs. Abernathy in 4C told me that her son Martin is back in town. And I told her you'd love to meet him. Would you give her a call? She says he'd loved to meet you too."

A perfect example of Eustacia's poor taste: Martin Abernathy was four years older than Lucy. He had a habit of snorting all the time and when she was little, he used to stick gum in her hair.

She rolled her eyes as her neighbour's shrill voice continued. She washed the dishes and put them away, and Eustacia was *still* talking. Then, finally making her excuses, Lucy hung up the phone and got ready for work.

Her clothing and shoes were comfortable, cosy and most importantly, breathable. There was a *lot* of walking around in her line of work, and no matter what the deodorant companies claimed, she'd rather be safe than sorry.

Dogs were after all, very sensitive to smell.

CHAPTER 2

First, Lucy headed to Olympus Avenue, where one of her charges resided.

While the service was called 12 Dogs, in truth she rarely had as many pooches all at once, but could certainly handle that much.

She also didn't do favourites, and would never admit to having one. Much like people, breeds were individual, and to say you liked dog one better than the other was somewhat unfair. People couldn't help who they were and neither could animals.

However, if Lucy *truly* had to choose a favourite dog – and was absolutely pressed on the matter – she'd pick Berry Cole.

Berry was a five-year-old chocolate brown Labrador and Great Dane mix – a Labradane.

Lucy just called him a sweetie.

He was loyal and loving, and despite his humongous

size, being closer in build to his Great Dane mother than his Lab father, he was very gentle.

He was also the perfect choice for his owner, Mrs Cole. Though Lucy sometimes wondered how the seventy-five-year-old woman managed to feed the colossus.

He was *always* hungry, so much so that Lucy had started carrying extra snacks soon after he'd joined her troop.

Though if she could pick a dog for herself, it couldn't be one as huge as Berry. But that was a moot point because unfortunately, Lucy's landlord didn't allow pets in the building.

Mrs Cole was a widow with no children, and Lucy sometimes wondered if that would be her own fate - a life alone. Though at least Mrs. Cole had a canine companion. She didn't even have that.

Now she knocked on the door.

"Morning," Mrs. Cole greeted Lucy with a smile the moment she opened the door. She looked tired today, more so than on most mornings when she called to pick up Berry.

Maybe she was feeling down.

Lucy could bring her back something from Toasties to perk up her spirits. It was the best cafe and pastry store in all of Whitedale, and Mrs Cole had a thing for their Peppermint Chocolate Croissants.

"Hi, Mrs. Cole. Is he ready?" The words came out in a plume of white. Winter was well and truly here and Christmas now only a couple of weeks away.

They'd had their first heavy snowfall just a few days before and soon, the entirety of Whitedale would be covered in it.

The words had only just left Lucy's mouth when the big dog came bounding to the door. He rushed past his owner and promptly jumped up and landed his big paws on her chest, knocking her back a step.

"Berry, calm down," Mrs. Cole scolded lightly.

"It's okay," Lucy laughed as Berry licked her face. "He's just happy to see me."

The older woman chuckled. "He always is. I can't contend with him like I used to with this hip. I'm so happy he still gets to go out and have fun when you're around."

"It's my pleasure, and you know I love this big guy," Lucy chuckled as she removed his paws from her chest and stooped down to scratch behind his ears.

Mrs. Cole duly handed her the leash from by the door and Lucy clipped it in place. She carried spare leashes and clean-up items in her backpack, but it was important to get Berry on the right track from the get-go.

"He's staying out for the whole day, yes?" she confirmed.

"Yes, if that's good with you."

Mrs. Cole was one of the few people Lucy could chat easily with. She supposed it was because she reminded her so much of the grandmother who had raised her.

She didn't have anyone now though. A fact she was well used to, but whenever Christmas came around, it was just that little bit harder to bear.

"Of course. You have a great day," Lucy told Mrs Cole as she began to lead Berry from the porch. "And get back inside, it's cold out. We'll see you later."

"You too," the older woman called after her, chuckling as Lucy struggled to keep pace with the dog. "And don't let the big guy wear you out too much."

CHAPTER 3

The spirit of Christmas was well and truly in the air.

All the stores in town were now fully decorated for the holiday season. Garlands and wreaths were everywhere, twinkling lights in every shop window, and the local tree farm business was booming with a fine selection of firs, pines and spruces.

Lucy wasn't getting a tree though. She never did. It felt wasted when it was just her.

She stopped for a moment to look into the window of Daphne's Dreamland Toy store, smiling automatically at the holiday display. The place was every child's wonderland and had been in existence for over forty years.

Lucy could remember when her mother used to bring her there as a child. The owner, Daphne would give her candy canes whenever she came in.

She was gone now though, just like Lucy's mother.

A deep sadness filled her heart at the memory. Her

mom had been a lone parent and her dad was in the military.

They married before being deployed but he never came back. He sent her mother annulment papers a few months later. He'd met someone else where he was stationed and decided that she was the better choice.

Her mother had never quite gotten over it.

A sudden jerk snapped Lucy back to the present as Berry resumed his march toward home.

It was now a little after four in the afternoon when she usually dropped the dogs back.

Berry was her final drop-off today, and he seemed to know it was past time because he was trotting toward Olympus so purposefully that she knew only the prospect of food could be drawing him.

"Hey, slow down there, buddy," she commanded gently. "We'll be there soon."

She'd never seen him so determined. It was strange.

"Wait. I'm coming, I'm coming," Lucy called as he rushed to the corner and made a beeline for the street. He jerked hard and she almost tripped on the curb as the leash slipped from her hand, and the big dog ran off.

He disappeared down the street and she rushed after him.

"Hey there big guy …" Lucy heard a voice call out from nearby, and rushing round to Mrs Cole's, she stopped short.

A man, over six feet tall and dressed in jeans, a red plaid shirt, brown jacket and a hard hat, was standing outside the house.

Lucy had never seen him before, but clearly, Berry had.

The dog's paws were planted solidly on the man's chest and he was licking his face eagerly, as his tail wagged behind him. The guy, whoever he was, was laughing heartily at the affection.

Lucy watched the friendly moment like an intruder.

"Hey buddy, where's your mama today, huh? Where is she?" he was asking in a sing-song tone.

It was several seconds before he noticed her and turned to meet her gaze, but when he did Lucy's breath hitched.

He was so handsome. Square jaw with a dimple in his chin. A five o'clock shadow, tanned skin and the most brilliant blue eyes she'd ever seen. He wasn't any Martin Abernathy that was for sure. She could see dark brown hair peeking out from beneath the hat.

"Hello," he greeted with a smile, then nodded toward the house. "You looking for Mrs. Cole, too?"

Lucy couldn't speak for several seconds. She just stared at him. This was what always happened when handsome men spoke to her; she completely lost all sense. Her shyness took over and suddenly she became an incoherent nincompoop, her mind completely muddled.

Finally, she found her tongue before she embarrassed herself any further.

"Yes, returning Berry. I'm his dog walker."

He looked at her blankly for a second and then smiled. "Oh. Are you Lucy?"

She was shocked that he knew her name.

"Yes …" she stammered. "Who are you?"

He took several steps to close the gap between them and extended his hand with a dazzling smile.

"I'm Scott. Mrs. Cole's contractor. I just finished working on her roof."

Lucy took his hand. "I didn't know she had one," she replied.

"A roof?"

A second of anxiety struck her. "No … a contractor."

He chuckled. "I was just kidding."

Well done Lucy. Next time, try something simple like 'Nice to meet you'.

"Nice to meet you," she mumbled.

"Nice to finally meet you too," he replied as he drew his hand back. He looked at the house and then back to her. "Was she expecting you back now?"

Finally? What did that mean? Did he know her from somewhere? She was certain he couldn't. She'd certainly never seen him before.

Maybe Mrs. Cole had mentioned her. But why?

"Yes. I always bring Berry back around this time. When he stays out all day," she added quickly, when she realized that she hadn't answered.

Berry himself was already at the door scratching to be let in. As always the big guy was ravenous.

"Strange," Scott stated as he turned back to her. "I've been here for a while now, and she hasn't answered. I usually check in on her when I can. I don't like that she's all alone in winter, especially given the darker nights and cold weather. So I try to stop by now and again, just to make sure she's okay."

How sweet.

"She's probably just late getting back from the store or something," he shrugged.

But that didn't make sense to Lucy. Mrs Cole always made sure she was home when they got there.

She knew how Berry got by that hour of the day. His mind was solely on his dinner and if he didn't get it he got grumpy.

Something wasn't right.

"I have to go," Scott said then. "I've got a meeting with a client over on Hilliard. Could you tell her I stopped by and I'll pass back soon?"

Lucy nodded. "Sure." She turned and watched him walk back to his truck.

Berry attempted to follow him but Lucy grabbed a hold of his leash as he tried to gallop off. "Oh no, you don't Buster. Not this time."

Scott got into the truck and then turned back to wave in their direction as he drove off. "See you around, Lucy."

She waved back, still slightly dazed by the unexpected encounter. "See you around."

CHAPTER 4

*B*ut the minute Scott was out of sight, Lucy's thoughts loosened, and a niggling discomfort began to fill her stomach.

She turned back to the quiet house. There was no sound of Christmas music coming from inside. Mrs Cole loved this time of year and she always left festive music playing - even when she went out.

"Nope. Something's not right."

Lucy walked toward the door and took the steps two at a time. She rang the doorbell.

Nothing. She knocked. Still nothing.

"Mrs. Cole?" she called out. No answer.

She looked at Berry. He was scratching at the door and whining a little.

"Let's try the back …" Lucy mused, as she led him from the porch and around the side of the house to check the rear kitchen window.

Inside, everything was dark and quiet.

"This isn't at all like her …." she muttered to herself. She knocked on the back door too.

Still nothing.

"Maybe Mrs Stillman knows where she might be?" she mumbled to Berry, as she headed back out front and next door to the neighbour's house.

Mrs. Stillman was a cat lover. The sound of mewing greeted Lucy the second she stepped onto her property. She looked up at the box window and saw a marmalade tabby looking back at her as she approached the door and knocked.

The owner answered a few seconds later. Her face looked drawn and her red hair was slightly dishevelled. She looked down at Berry and her face fell.

"Hi, Mrs. Stillman. I was just over at Mrs Cole's to drop Berry back, but she doesn't seem to be home yet, which is unusual. Would you by any chance know where she is?"

The other woman's expression became more solemn by the second, and a further sense of foreboding began to slither into Lucy's heart.

The neighbor sighed. "I don't know how to tell you this Lucy, but Sonia passed away earlier today. I only just got back from the hospital."

Lucy's hearing had become hollow. The words being spoken weren't real. They didn't make sense.

Mrs. Cole couldn't be … *dead*.

She had only left her a few hours ago, smiling and fine. Yes, the older woman had mentioned she felt tired, but she seemed in good health.

How could she be dead?

"How ...?"

"We're not sure. They suspect that it may have been an aneurysm in her sleep," Mrs Stillman explained. "I went over earlier to drop off a pecan pie I'd made. She really loved my pecan pie," she added through tears.

Tears were filling Lucy's eyes too. She looked at Berry. His mama was gone, but of course he had no idea.

What was going to become of him?

"When I didn't hear her answer I knew something was wrong," Mrs. Stillman continued. "I called the ambulance right off. When we went in, she was in her bed in that nice floral dress she got a few weeks ago."

Lucy could only nod. If she tried to speak she'd start sobbing and she couldn't let herself do that.

It had been so long since she'd lost someone she cared about, and Mrs Cole's death hurt almost as much as her grandmother's had.

"Thank you for telling me, Mrs. Stillman." She forced the words from her lips. "I'll be going now."

The other woman nodded her understanding as Lucy turned to leave.

She couldn't believe this was happening. She walked back to the house and took a seat on the porch steps.

Berry sat beside her and promptly lay his big head in her lap. He looked up at her pleadingly.

"I know you're hungry Big Guy, but I can't get you food just yet," she told him. She stroked the top of his head gently. "You're mama's gone, buddy. Mrs. Cole won't be able to take care of you anymore."

21

Berry let out a whine as if he understood.

Lucy knew that science would say that he was just picking up on her emotions, but she guessed deep down that animals understood a great deal more than people gave them credit for.

CHAPTER 5

*L*ucy waited for over an hour for someone to come to the house, feeding Berry the remainder of the food she kept in her backpack.

The family of people who died usually came by to check on things, didn't they?

It was then she remembered that Mrs. Cole's niece, Joy, had moved to California a few months ago.

She had no family in town anymore. No one was coming.

What was she going to do with Berry?

Lucy walked back to Mrs Stillman's.

"Me again," she said as the other woman answered the door.

"Lucy, what are you still doing here?"

"I was waiting for someone from Mrs. Cole's family to come, so I can give them Berry, but then I remembered that Joy moved."

"Months ago."

"Right, that's the problem. There's nowhere for me to take him," she explained nervously.

"I see. What are you going to do?"

Lucy forced a smile as she gave Mrs Stillman a pleading look. "I was kind of hoping that maybe he could stay here for a bit …"

"No."

"Just for the night, even?"

"I'm sorry, but - "

"Please, Mrs. Stillman. He has nowhere to go. I'd take him home with me in a heartbeat, but animals aren't allowed in my building. He just needs someplace to spend the night. I promise tomorrow I'll find a more suitable situation. I promise." She raised three fingers in the air. "Brownie promise."

It was the best she could offer.

The other woman looked at her and then at Berry and then at the cat that was curling around her ankles.

"Fine, but just for the night. He can stay out back and I'll get some food from next door."

Lucy gave a huge internal sigh of relief. "Thank you."

"Just overnight," the woman insisted. "I don't like dogs, Lucy. They're too much trouble. Cats, they're inde-pendent. A lot easier to handle."

Lucy nodded. She didn't care what Mrs Stillman preferred as long as Berry had someplace to sleep tonight.

"I'll be back tomorrow morning, I swear."

"What time?"

"Is seven good for you?" she asked handing over Berry's leash and giving him a reassuring rub around the ears.

"Seven sharp."

"I'll be there."

CHAPTER 6

*N*ext, Lucy went to work on her landlord.

"Please Mr Wells. Mrs Cole is gone and Berry has no one to take care of him."

"What's that got to do with me?"

He was short and Lucy was sure, jealous of everything that could possibly be as tall as him. Which was why animals were a problem too. Their character was greater than his height.

"If you could bend the rule on pets in the building just this once, I could bring Berry here and take care of him until I can make arrangements with Mrs Cole's family."

"Absolutely not. If I bend it for you I have to bend it for everyone, and then my entire building is overrun with furballs and fleas. No, thank you."

"It won't be like that," she assured him.

"My answer is still no."

"Won't you reconsider - please? It's Christmas," Lucy asked, but the look on his face made her stop.

He wasn't changing his mind for her or anyone, no matter what time of the year it was.

She'd just have to find another way.

Berry was too large for her apartment anyway. He deserved a big house and garden, like Mrs Cole's, where he could run around and have space.

She went to pick up Berry at seven just as she promised.

Mrs Stillman looked frazzled.

She informed Lucy that Berry had whined all night and she'd hardly slept a wink.

Even worse, it had upset all of her six cats and they'd done a number on her couch in response.

Lucy couldn't apologize enough as she took the leash from her and led Berry away. The further away they both were, the better.

She'd figure something out.

SHE THEN TOOK Berry and her other charges for their usual walk to McGivney Park.

It was one of the few places they could be off their leashes, and all the dogs loved it there.

Once they arrived, Lucy unhooked their collars and let them run around and have fun while she sat on a nearby bench watching.

The only one who wasn't allowed off-leash was Pegasus. The black and white Japanese Chin had a habit of running away.

She didn't like playing with the other dogs and Lucy

was convinced that it was because Pegasus thought herself better than running around in a park.

She looked at the other dogs with such an air of condescension it was always better to keep her close.

She and Perdita, Mr. Cross's Dalmatian, were always yapping at each other. Perdita didn't like Pegasus one bit and more often than not, Lucy had to act the go-between.

Now, she put her phone to her ear again as she tried to sort out her most pressing problem.

"Hello? Is this Joy?" Lucy had called every Joy Reese she could find in the directory until she finally reached the right one.

"Yes."

"You don't know me, but I'm Lucy Adams. I take care of Berry the dog, for your aunt, Mrs. Cole." She nodded solemnly as Joy explained that her aunt had passed away. "Yes, I know. That's why I called. You see, Berry is going to need someplace to live and I was hoping that you could take him."

"I can't," the woman replied quickly.

Lucy's heart sank. "May I ask why not?"

"Look, my aunt loved that dog but I don't. I don't do pets and I have no intention of taking on such a responsibility. And that dog is HUGE."

"I know he's on the bigger side, but truly, Berry is such a sweetie that you'd have no trouble at all."

"I don't think you understand. I don't want to try. I just don't want a dog. It doesn't work for me, or my lifestyle."

Lucy's heart was plummeting rapidly every second that went by. "So what should I do with him?"

"I don't know to be honest. Sorry, but I have my aunt's funeral to prepare for at the moment. I can't deal with what's going to happen to some dog. I'm sorry, but I can't help you."

With that, the line disconnected and Lucy stared blankly at her phone, shocked. She couldn't believe the stance Joy had taken to the idea of caring for Berry.

He was such a wonderful dog. How could she feel that way about him - how could anyone?

Lucy knew that the woman's feelings were shared by many others in the world, but she'd never personally experienced anyone express such outright dislike before.

She was quite stunned, frankly. But still, the problem remained. What was she going to do now?

There was no choice.

Clearly, it was up to Lucy to find Berry a new home, and soon.

CHAPTER 7

*L*ater, she took the other dogs back to their owners, and then took Berry along to Toasties.

They had free wifi and Lucy used that and Betsy her PC to make up some fliers. It took her several tries to get the wording just the way she wanted, but in the end, she was pleased with her efforts.

"What do you think?" she asked as she turned the screen for Berry to see. He raised his nose and sniffed the laptop before losing interest. "What? You don't like it?"

Lucy finished her snack and then emailed the flier to the print shop, ordering up a batch of thirty.

She'd pick them up and plaster them around town.

Hopefully, some prospects would give her a call and Berry would have a new home sooner rather than later.

The print shop had her copies ready by the time she arrived. She'd used festive graphics and snapped a cute picture of Berry, wanting the flier to stand out.

No one was going to miss it.

Lucy began to staple fliers on every pole and post in town she could find. She asked a few store owners if she could post some in their windows and they allowed her to do so.

"Hey, what's that?" a boy asked as she stapled her last to a lamp post.

"It's a flier."

"For what?" He had to be about five. A curious age.

Lucy stooped down to his height.

"It's to try and find a home for this dog," she explained as Berry moved closer.

He stretched his head forward to sniff the boy but the little kid recoiled.

"Don't worry. He won't hurt you," Lucy assured him.

"He's so big," he gasped in wonder. "He must cost a lot of money."

"Actually, I'm not selling him; I'm giving him away to whoever can give him a good home," she explained.

"Why?" the boy asked. "Don't you like him?"

She chuckled. "I like him a lot, but he's not mine. The lady who owned him sadly died so now he needs a home. I have to find a new owner for him in time for Christmas."

"That's sad. My dog Ruffles died too. What's his name?"

"He's Berry," Lucy continued as she patted his side gently. "He's a Labradane."

"A what?"

She started to laugh just as a tall blonde woman called out. "Tobey?"

"Is that your mom?" Lucy asked gently. The smile was still teasing her lips.

He nodded.

"I think she's calling you. You should probably go to her."

The boy smiled. He was missing a front tooth. He took off running.

"Mommy! Mommy! That lady over there is giving away a dog for Christmas. Can I have him?"

But by the outright horrified look on his mom's face at the dog's size, Lucy was certain little Tobey, and unfortunately, Berry too, was on to a loser.

THE FLIERS DISAPPEARED FASTER than expected and soon, Lucy was exhausted.

"Let's see how it goes overnight," she told Berry as he trotted skittishly beside her. "You never know who might see them. If we don't have any luck, then I'll order up a few more and head further outside of town."

Berry barked happily and Lucy wished it was because he agreed, but she knew it was probably only because he wanted the snack in her pocket.

She took one out and tossed it to him when her phone rang.

Lucy didn't recognize the number. "Hello? Yes, this *is* who you call about the dog," she repeated cheerfully, giving Berry an excited smile. "Yes, of course, you can. Are you free now?"

The call was short but to the point. The Emersons

from Crichton Corner were looking for a dog and saw her flier in one of the shop windows just now. They were interested in Berry.

Excitement filled her chest as she began to walk in the direction of Taylor's Arts and Things.

The family had been buying supplies for their daughter's school project when they saw the flier. They were a young couple with a child, which was perfect. Labradanes were family dogs and great with children.

Lucy was very hopeful that the Emersons might be the answer to her prayers.

She saw them immediately as she approached.

Mrs. Emerson was a few inches shorter than her husband. They were both blondes, fair-skinned and wrapped up snuggly in matching plaid scarves.

"Mr. and Mrs. Emerson," she greeted with a smile as she got closer.

"Lucy?"

"Yes. And this is Berry," she said as she and Berry got closer.

Mrs. Emerson's eyes grew to twice the size.

"This is … it?" She looked at her husband.

Lucy frowned. "Is something wrong?"

"Not really, it's just … we thought he would be smaller," she said. Her speech was stilted and Lucy was confused.

"Haven't you ever seen a Labradane before?"

"No, we just saw the picture on the flier and thought he looked sweet," she explained. "I'm sorry. We live in a small house with no backyard. We don't have the space."

"We're really sorry to have bothered you," her husband added, smiling pitifully. "Thanks for coming."

Lucy's hopes were falling off a cliff, and that was all he had to say?

It wasn't his fault though, she thought disheartened.

Maybe she should've put something in the picture to give people an idea of his size.

Sadly, Lucy couldn't think of anything that could convey the dog's big heart too.

CHAPTER 8

Two more days passed and still Lucy had no luck in her quest, other than getting a break from Mrs. Stillman who'd agreed to let the big dog stay with her a little longer, but only at night.

It wasn't long before more people noticed the fliers though.

The town was small and some already knew Berry as being Mrs. Cole's dog, and were keen to take him in given his sweet temperament, but once Lucy met with such prospects she realized that the trouble wasn't him, so much as it was them.

Most didn't have the space for a dog his size. Others weren't up to his care, or they couldn't afford the cost associated with such a large (and hungry) breed.

She was surprised that there was even one who had an issue with Lucy not being able to provide papers to ensure the purity of Berry's parents.

Others were like Mrs Cole, older and infirm. Not ideal.

She'd endured repeated hopes and repeated let-downs and was beyond frustrated by the time she finished talking to the Ruprechts.

They were nice people, but were planning a move in a few months, and given they were relocating to Denver City, it didn't make sense.

They'd merely find themselves in the same position Lucy was now. Such a temporary arrangement wasn't fair to Berry.

Now, Lucy was dreading having to go back to Mrs Stillman to ask for even more time, but she had no choice.

Mrs Cole's neighbour was waiting for her when she arrived. The look on her face was laced with disapproval.

"I take it that you still haven't found a place?"

Lucy shook her head despondently. "No. I tried. They were good people, but just not the right fit."

"I can tell you what's not the right fit – that dog in my house. I've lost two lamps already. I'll have to remove the carpet in the back room where he sleeps, and honestly, my cats are so unnerved that it's driving me nuts. I can't keep him anymore, Lucy. I'm sorry. I really am, but I can't do it anymore. Christmas is on the way and my house is a disaster zone. I can't clean it because of that … *beast*, and my family's going to be arriving for the holidays soon. He has to go."

"Please Mrs. Stillman, just give me a few more days. Like you say, Christmas is on the way and Berry needs a home in time for then - the right home. I still have a few more leads," she pleaded.

"This is it, Lucy. Absolute last time. You get three days, and then he's out of here, or I take him to the shelter myself. I mean it." She took the leash from Lucy who watched as a sorrowful-looking Berry disappeared inside.

Clearly, he was enjoying his stay here just as much as Mrs. Stillman.

Three days?

Lucy couldn't - *wouldn't* - consider the local shelter. It just wasn't and had never been an option. She loved the big guy too much and could never abandon him that way.

But what was she supposed to do?

Lucy was fast becoming all out of options.

CHAPTER 9

*S*unset Trail was the most picturesque spot in Whitedale and perfect for dog-walking.

It was why Lucy liked going there so much. Lots of quiet space and room to roam between the trees, along the meandering landscape and with a view of Treasure Lake that was unsurpassed.

Sunlight reflected on beautiful blue water like diamonds and gold, which was how it got its name.

Set on a gentle winding slope, the trail was a criss-cross of paths along Lonesome Ridge, Whitedale's diminutive mountain.

Every day she took the dogs there, weather permitting; the park being for days when the forecast wasn't so great or the likelihood of rain was imminent.

Though right now Lucy felt as if she was walking under a cloud, but at least the weather was clear.

There was absolutely no one left on her prospects list.

Mrs. Stillman was adamant that Berry was going to

have to leave soon and there was no place else for Lucy to put him.

She'd gone back to her landlord again, begging him, but that was a waste of time. The local vet couldn't help either; none of his regulars were looking for a new dog and he wasn't prepared to even temporarily house an animal of Berry's size.

She was well and truly stuck.

Oscar, Mr. Reese's Alsatian was trotting beside her. Perdita was jumping all over her new boyfriend Pongo. Mrs Cross figured her precious lady was lonely and thought it a good idea to get her someone to play with. She needed to hold back a little on the whole *101 Dalmatians* thing.

Lucy's mind was so cluttered. She wanted to keep Berry in town, someplace he knew, someplace where the landscape was familiar.

There had to be *something* she could do to help.

Her thoughts were so scattered that she didn't realize she'd wandered off their usual path. It was only when snowflakes began to fall that she glanced up to see that it was darker than it should be.

The trees seemed much closer now, and the overhanging foliage thicker; blocking out the light.

It was then Lucy realized that she was on unfamiliar terrain. With all her musing, she'd allowed the dogs to lead her deeper into the woods.

A sense of panic began to rise in her stomach now, as the cold wind sliced through the trees, making her shiver a little.

"Where are we guys?" she mumbled.

Lucy looked in every direction, but nothing seemed familiar, and she couldn't tell which way the lake was, finding it even harder to get her bearings.

The dogs hovered around her. They wanted to keep going but she didn't know which direction they should turn.

Maybe if we just go back the way we came?

She turned to do so, but at this point couldn't figure out which direction they'd come here from.

This was ... not good.

"Keep calm Lucy. Nothing to worry about. You just need to keep walking. You'll find something," she told herself.

Trying to use her cell phone was pointless; there was no signal on this trail - another reason it was so perfect. You could escape the outside world while you were there, and just enjoy the scenery and the quiet solitude.

But of course that wasn't much help to her now.

She was at a loss when Berry suddenly turned to the right and barked.

Lucy's gaze snapped in the direction he was looking.

"What? Is there something over there?"

The big dog barked again and began to pull away from her, his tail wagging rapidly now.

Well, if there was something over there that had him reacting in that way, then like it or not, they were going in that direction.

Lead the way, Big Dog.

CHAPTER 10

*T*he snow began to fall harder as Lucy and the other dogs hurried along with Berry leading the way.

The older ones were amusing themselves by jumping on one another and sniffing the unfamiliar territory.

All Lucy wanted was to see something she recognized. Once she did she'd feel as happy and carefree as they were.

She checked her watch. If she didn't find a way back soon, the owners would be unhappy. She was always right on time dropping back their pets. Timekeeping was important to her, and them.

If she was very late dropping them back today, how was she going to explain it? What effect would it have on her business?

When Lucy was scared of one thing suddenly there seemed to be a million more things to worry about as well.

She was still following Berry when something glinted in the distance.

Lucy squinted and tried to make out what it was. It took her a minute to realize it was the sun reflecting on a window.

Relief swept over her. If there was a window, then there was a house. If there was a house, then maybe there was someone home.

Someone who could point them in the right direction.

The second the house came into view, Berry began to bark more. He ran toward it as if it were calling him.

Lucy couldn't hold on to him and all the others too.

The dogs' combined strength was a lot to deal with, especially when Berry was so eager. He'd excited the pack, and the task of calming them all wasn't something she needed right now.

Besides, she could see where he was going, so she figured she might as well just let him lead the way.

Releasing him off the leash, Lucy hurried the other animals along behind Berry. The snow was really coming down now. At least the house would be a good place to shelter for a bit if nothing else.

They broke through the trees into a clearing around the property. The first thing that struck Lucy was the state of the building. It looked abandoned, though the house itself wasn't dilapidated.

Why would anyone leave a nice place in such a gorgeous location unattended?

The site had an uninterrupted view of the lake, and

there wasn't another home to be found as far as the eye could see.

It was double-height, lodge-cabin style; a combination of stone and wood. A gabled roof and huge window panes maximized the natural light and the beautiful surroundings.

The land around it was cleared, as if the owner intended to put in a lawn or maybe a flowerbed, but there was nothing there now.

To one side was a deck that extended out into a jetty on the water.

It was Lucy's dream house.

She walked closer and quickly realized that the place wasn't abandoned like she'd first thought. It was in fact, under construction. The roof on the far side of the porch was half completed.

And perfect for sheltering beneath out of the snow, at least for now.

"Come on guys," Lucy urged as she began to jog to the house.

The dogs followed happily as they tried to keep up.

By now she was cold and her breath was coming out as a white mist with every exhalation.

"Berry!" she called as she got closer. "Wait, hold on!"

Of course, the big guy didn't wait and instead raced around the side of the house.

Lucy safely secured the other dogs to a nearby post before going in search of him.

There was construction material lying around everywhere, stuff that she didn't have the first clue about, but her primary focus was finding Berry.

"Berry, come here boy," she called out again.

Then a sound from somewhere nearby caught her attention and she walked around the porch to find Berry standing over someone lying on the ground; the dog's face buried in their neck, and his tail wagging a mile-a-minute.

"Berry!"

For a moment she was horrified, but then realized that the person's hands weren't fending the dog off, but rubbing his coat and scratching his fur.

And when that person turned in the direction of her voice, Lucy realized to her surprise that she recognized who it was.

CHAPTER 11

"Scott?'

The same dazzling eyes that had so befuddled her that first day they met, now turned in Lucy's direction, having the same effect on her as they did the first time.

Berry noticed her then too, and the big pooch came bounding back to her.

She laid a calming hand on his back as he panted by her side.

Scott pushed up from the ground, covered in what looked like sawdust and with a big smile on his face.

"Lucy, what are you doing here?" he asked as he dusted himself off.

"I could ask you the same thing," she replied reattaching Berry's leash and keeping a firm grip on it.

Scott's presence explained at least why the big dog had been so drawn to the house. He'd obviously picked up the scent of his friend from the trees.

Thank goodness.

"I live here," he answered and chuckled when Lucy glanced sceptically at the house. "I know, it's a mess. Who could live here, right? I mean, it's my place, but I haven't moved in permanently - not yet. The house is still under construction as you can probably tell. I've been working on it for about a year now."

"By yourself?" Lucy couldn't betray her surprise. The thought that he'd done all this on his own was impressive.

"Yes. I started the construction as a pet project and I'd hoped to have it done a long time ago, but business picked up and I had so much work backing up for other people that it sort of got put on ice." He looked at the house and gave a rueful smile.

"It's a really beautiful place. Anyone would love to live here."

"You think so?"

"Definitely. I would for sure," she added with a nervous chuckle, then coughed when she realized how weird that may have sounded.

Thankfully the sound of the other pooches' impatient whining drew their attention.

"Do you have more dogs with you?" Scott asked as he and Lucy moved back toward the porch.

"Yes. I'm sorry to intrude. I was walking them in the woods and we got lost. Berry is the one who led us here. I tied the others to the porch so I could go look for him," she explained.

The snowfall was thickening quickly as they stepped

back onto the porch and the dogs were circling agitatedly. They could feel the bad weather coming, Lucy suspected.

She needed to get them home.

"Could you tell me the fastest way to get back to town from here?" she asked Scott, as he headed toward the others and stooped to greet them, patting their heads and rubbing their coats.

They were all friendly dogs who welcomed strangers and seemed *very* pleased with Scott's attention.

And by the delighted look on his face, clearly, the feeling was mutual.

He glanced up at the sky. "There's no going back to town until the weather clears, and certainly not on foot," he stated. "This isn't going to let up anytime soon."

Lucy looked pained. "So we're stuck?"

"Looks like it," he replied. "Weather changes quickly up on the trail. Usually doesn't last long, but a cold snap can lead to some serious snowfall, and it is that time of year. You guys are welcome to stay here until it passes, though."

"Oh no, we couldn't impose ..." Lucy protested.

"Don't be silly, it's no imposition. If anything you'd be doing me a favor."

"How so?"

"If you stay and shelter here, you make me feel better knowing that guys are safe. Plus, if you do, I can give you a ride back when the worst clears."

The proposition was tempting, and the thought of

making their way back to town in this snow wasn't one Lucy relished.

Chances were there was cellphone reception at Scott's house too, so she could keep the owners informed of their pets' whereabouts.

Plus Lucy kind of wanted to see what the inside of the house looked like.

"Okay," she conceded, smiling gratefully. "Thank you."

CHAPTER 12

Scott welcomed them all inside the house, leading Lucy to an enclosed rear room that was unfinished, but insulated from the outside.

She settled the dogs there before following him in to the kitchen which was partially furnished, but seemed fully operational.

"Hot chocolate?" he asked as he approached the stove. He turned on a burner and placed a small pot over the flame.

"Yes, please. I love hot chocolate."

She watched as Scott poured heavy cream into the pot and dropped several chunks of chocolate into it. He added several other things too but she couldn't tell what they were.

"Please don't go to any trouble - I thought you meant the powdered kind," she insisted, watching him work.

"Not in this house. My mom was the kind of woman who liked to make things from scratch," he smiled as he stirred the contents. "She taught me well. Marshmallows?"

Lucy couldn't help but smile. "Is it even hot chocolate if there isn't?"

When the chocolate was ready, Scott poured it into two large mugs and set one on the table in front of her, adding several huge marshmallows on top. "Enjoy."

She sipped the warm, creamy liquid and hummed her approval. "It's delicious."

"Thanks. Mom's recipe."

"So is she going to live with you here too?" she queried conversationally.

"No. She died a few years ago."

"I'm so sorry."

"It's OK," he assured her easily. "How about you? Does your family live in town?"

"No," Lucy confessed. "It's just me. I don't have any family."

"I know how that is." He raised his mug to her and winked. "I guess here's to us loners then."

"Cheers."

"How is Mrs. Cole?" he asked, as he sipped his chocolate. They were sitting facing each other at the table and Lucy almost spit out her chocolate at the question.

"You mean you haven't heard?" Sadness reared up inside her afresh.

"Heard what?" Scott asked with a hint of alarm.

"Poor Mrs Cole died last week."

The expression on his face was nothing short of stunned.

"I … had no idea. I was supposed to come back but I've been working flat out nearly every day coming up to the holidays. I was actually planning to go see her tomorrow. I can't believe it."

"She passed the day I met you," Lucy informed him. "An aneurysm, apparently."

"I can't believe it. She was such a sweet old lady and so tough. I kinda thought she'd live forever."

"I know." Lucy felt fresh tears brim at the corner of her eyes.

"So what's going to happen to Berry?" he asked, and she wished he hadn't reminded her of that all too pressing problem.

"I have no idea," she said sighing. "I've been trying so hard to find someone to take him since then, but I've run out of options. He's been with Mrs. Stillman up to now, but she can't handle him anymore. She says I have a couple more days and after that, he's out."

"No one wants to adopt an awesome dog like Berry?" Scott asked, surprised.

"No, that's just it. There were some people interested, but they weren't suitable. They didn't have enough space or they were too old, or simply hadn't thought it through."

"You really care about him."

"Of course I do. He's a great dog, and such a sweetie too, as you know. I love taking care of him. Mrs Cole loved him, and that's why I need to make sure he goes to someone she'd approve of. I can't just give him to anyone. I need to make sure he'd be happy."

She'd run off on a tangent. It happened sometimes. Now, Scott was just staring at her with a thoughtful look on his face.

"So no one's good enough," he said as he sipped his chocolate again.

Lucy blushed. "I guess so. It's just, that I'd hate for him to go to someone who wouldn't love him as Mrs. Cole did. Someone who wouldn't treat him right. I haven't been successful yet, but I'm sure I'm going to find someone, the perfect someone for him."

"I understand. I have a few rescues myself I'm hoping to rehome with the right people, but I haven't had a chance to start looking yet."

Lucy looked up, interested. "Rescue dogs?"

"Yes, four little guys I came across while on the job. Lou Lou, I found down on Weston. She's an American English Coonhound I saw wandering the woods a few weeks ago. She didn't have a collar or any way to identify her, so I think she may have belonged to some hunters who left her behind. Some people just don't care for their pets the way they should."

"I know. I can't stand it. I just don't understand how you can treat any living thing with such disrespect." Lucy smiled then. "That breed's a really sweet animal too. Very amiable."

"I know," Scott grinned. "Whenever she sees me, it's like coming home to a friend."

"She's here?" Lucy asked, surprised. She hadn't seen any animals when she came in and wondered where they were.

"I have a kennel out back. I built it because I hope to one day get some Leonbergers, or maybe a Neapolitan Mastiff."

Lucy's heart was backflipping in her chest. Neapolitan Mastiffs? They were such huge, beautiful animals. She'd always wanted to see one up close but had never had the chance. They were also very expensive dogs and required a lot of care.

"Well, whenever you do get them I'd love to be your walker," she offered genuinely.

"I'll keep that in mind."

"So, you were telling me about Lou Lou?" Lucy got back to the topic at hand. "You know, in terms of rehoming her, a dog like that needs someone who can help stimulate its hunting nature. It wouldn't be fair to have her cooped up in a house. You wouldn't want a novice having her either. Breaking her in, if she's not already broken, will be a lot of trouble for someone who doesn't know what they're doing. Coonhounds are stubborn and tenacious. They take a little working with, but once they're settled they're just perfect."

He grinned. "You really know a lot about dogs, don't you?"

"Yes," she chuckled bashfully. "I once thought of studying to be a vet when I moved back home from the city, but I gave that idea up pretty quickly. Being a dog walker works best for me right now, but once I get everything in order you'll see. I have big plans for 12 Dogs."

Scott chuckled. "I don't doubt that for a second."

"So what else are you keeping out there?"

"Well, there's ET, a male Kelpie."

Lucy tried not to laugh at the names Scott had given his rescues. "A good dog, but they get lonely very quickly. Needs someone who can be with them as much as possible. It's a working dog, bred to be active. Shouldn't be kept inside, and needs to get lots of exercise. I mean *lots*."

Scott kept grinning at her as she espoused the traits of each breed, and who would be the most suitable owner for them.

"You're good at that you know, matching dogs to the right kind of people."

Lucy shrugged. "I guess. I just know my breeds."

"Have you ever heard of a place called Lisdoonvarna?"

"No. Where is that? Slovakia?"

"Ireland. They have a festival there every summer called the Lisdoonvarna Matchmaking Festival. It's apparently Europe's biggest singles event. Great fun."

"You've been?" Lucy asked, mostly surprised that Scott might be single.

"Yes, earlier this year. Some friends and I were there for a vacation and heard about it. It's been going on for over a hundred and sixty years."

"That's a long time."

"It is. They have this matchmaker guy who, the myth says, if you touch his book with both hands you'll be married within six months." Scott chuckled and drained his mug. "I don't know about that though."

"What? You don't believe that stuff like that can happen?"

"Not really. It's nice to think and to hope for, but I think you and I would have better luck hitting one of the bars." He grinned.

Lucy was intrigued. Then her eyes grew wide. What was he suggesting? Was Scott implying that she needed to go out and get matched?

Suddenly she was embarrassed and uncomfortable again.

"So what does that have to do with me?" she asked hesitantly.

"You could be Whitedale's matchmaker. But instead of people, you could match dogs to potential owners. Turn it into something fun."

There was a novel thought. A dog matchmaking service? It would certainly be a unique addition to her business. And unlike her matchmaking neighbour Eustasia, Lucy understood her customer at least.

Also felt nice that Scott thought she had a talent.

The problem was, Lucy thought ruefully, at the moment she couldn't seem to utilise it for poor Berry.

Or could she?

CHAPTER 13

"So how do you think I should I go about something like this … for Berry, I mean?" she asked thoughtfully.

She liked what Scott was saying, but the mechanics of it was the question.

"Well," he sat forward in his seat. "I guess you begin like you've just done verbally with me - come up with a kind of … profile, like a dating profile, listing Berry's canine personality traits, and a corresponding list of preferable qualities in an owner. And maybe my brood too, if you wanted to make a thing of it."

She nodded. "But how do I let people know about it?" She didn't relish the idea of posting up more fliers all around town.

"Well, Christmas is the perfect time to get the whole community interested and involved. You could maybe even open a booth or something."

"12 Dogs of Christmas…" Lucy's brain suddenly kicked into high gear.

"Yes, perfect. I love it! See, you *are* good at this stuff."

Suddenly, she was on a roll. "We can clean Berry and the dogs up, maybe put a bow and some festive ribbons on them and take some photos for their profiles. Set up a doggie matchmaking service to find them their forever homes in time for Christmas. A booth at the Christmas fair would be perfect."

"Yes," Scott was nodding enthusiastically. "All those people in one place all at once. If not from here, then maybe even McKinley? Every year people come over for the tree-lighting ceremony. Lots of potential matches. Our own matchmaking festival here in Whitedale, except for dogs."

The grin on Lucy's face wouldn't subside. She *loved* this idea. And, most importantly, it truly could be the perfect opportunity to find Berry *his* perfect match in time for the holidays. Scott's ingenuity had once again set a fire under her and motivated her to keep going.

But what was she going to do with him in the mean-time? Lucy remembered then, suddenly crestfallen once more.

The Christmas fair was days away, and she still needed somewhere to keep him.

"Sounds great in theory, but what do I do with Berry until then?" she mused out loud.

Scott shrugged. "Why don't I keep him here?"

"You?"

"Yes, why not? I have plenty of space, plus I already

know Berry. And I think he likes me. We get along pretty well, don't you think?"

She smiled. "That you do."

"Can I get you a refill?" he asked, as he got to his feet with his mug in hand.

"No thanks, I'd better get going," Lucy looked at her watch, suddenly realizing the time. Scott was so easy and interesting to talk to the time seemed to have just flown by.

She looked out the window; the snowfall had eased, but the sun was disappearing fast. "I have to get the dogs home …" She jumped to her feet.

"Right," Scott replied. "That's a shame. I almost forgot you were on the job."

"Me too." She gave him a rueful smile. "It was nice of you to let us stay this long."

"My pleasure," he answered as he washed the mugs and set them on the drainer. Then he shook the water from his hands and grabbed a towel to dry them. "Let's get you guys home."

BEFORE THEY LEFT, Scott took Berry out back to the kennel he'd told Lucy about, and to introduce her to the other dogs he'd rescued.

It was a big area with plenty of space for them all to run around in, and the kennels themselves were heated and spacious. It was perfect for the big dog and a life-saver for Lucy. And Mrs Stillman too, no doubt.

She stooped down beside Berry to say goodbye, and he licked her face happily.

"I've got to go now buddy," Lucy said hugging him gently. "Scott's going to take care of you for a little while, but I promise I'll come back to visit you," she said, then looked up at Scott, a little embarrassed for assuming. "If that's OK?"

He smiled. "I wouldn't have it any other way."

CHAPTER 14

*T*he following morning, Lucy woke with sunshine on her face.

Not literally, but it felt that way.

Thanks to Scott's idea and his kind offer to help Berry, she had a spring in her step and a huge weight off her mind.

She bounded out of bed, did her stretches and never had a better-tasting bowl of cereal. She finger-combed her hair into a high ponytail and brushed her teeth while dancing to cheery Christmas songs on the radio.

As expected, Mrs Stillman was over the moon to learn that Berry would no longer be an occupant of her house. The timing was perfect too because her family had called to inform her that they'd be coming for the holidays a day earlier, leaving her with no choice but to boot him out.

Disaster averted, just in time.

· · ·

LUCY PICKED up her usual charges for their walk and the morning seemed to go by quicker, but that might've been because she was so inspired and eager to get cracking with Scott's dog matchmaking idea.

It was such a brainwave, and sure to be fun, too.

By lunchtime, things had already started to fall into place. She called the town's fair committee and spoke to Mary Winter, the overly enthusiastic community organizer who loved all things Christmas.

Mary was always the first one in town to hang out decorations, and she prided herself on having 'the best' Christmas Cookies on sale at the fair. They were, too.

Lucy was over the moon at her response to the idea of the matchmaking booth. She also happened to be one of the world's biggest dog lovers, so the idea of helping some down-on-their-luck pups find a home for Christmas was something Mary was deeply enthusiastic about.

"12 Dogs of Christmas is a *great* name for a booth, Lucy. I love it!" she cooed delightedly.

So, she had the permission she needed. But now, Lucy had some groundwork to do.

Berry would be happy at Scott's place for a couple of days, a fantastic temporary solution.

She was determined to have a happy home for him soon and was also enjoying the prospect of helping Scott out in return.

You really had to love dogs to pick up and take care of strays, not to mention assume the responsibility of rehoming them.

And Lucy really wanted to help him find his rescues their forever homes. He'd already done a lot for these pups by taking them in and caring for them.

It showed real heart.

Once she'd dropped all the dogs back that afternoon, she picked up her cell and dialled the number Scott had given her the night before, giddily pacing her kitchen as she told him about her progress thus far.

And when he suggested she come by his place to plan things further, visit Berry and take him for his walk, Lucy couldn't deny that she was equally enthused about seeing them both.

CHAPTER 15

*I*t took her a little while to find her way back to Scott's this time, which was around the back of Lonesome Ridge.

Lucy still couldn't believe she'd wandered so far off the path as to find her way to his house in the first place.

Thank goodness for Berry and his sensitive nose.

The house was even more stunning in full daylight against a clear blue sky.

Scott had finished a project earlier that week thus was home again, working on the house.

"Hey there," Lucy called out as she got out of her red Chevy pick-up. He turned and waved at her from the roof, a bright smile lighting up his handsome features.

"I see you found your way back on wheels this time."

"Yep, better prepared," she chuckled as she watched him climb down a ladder.

"You want to see Berry and the others first?" he asked. "Give you a chance to get to know them a little."

"That'd be great."

"So how's your day been?" he asked as they walked side-by-side to the rear of the property.

"Couldn't be better," Lucy replied. "I was out earlier and my thoughts were going a mile a minute. I really can't thank you enough for suggesting the matchmaking idea. It's genius."

"Don't mention it. You're helping me too, so it's a win-win situation. I can't keep my guys here forever, and until the house is done I can't give them the attention they deserve. They need more than just visits to feed and walk them. They need a home with someone who loves them and can give them what they need. Just like you said."

He led her to the kennels where Berry, Lou Lou and ET were happily running around the holding area.

As they drew closer, Lucy thought she could hear the faint sound of yelping.

"What's that?" she asked. "Did you get puppies?"

"Found them on my way back from work earlier. A box left on the side of the highway on my way back from McKinley. "Akitas."

"Someone just left them on the road to die?" Lucy exclaimed, appalled.

"Looks that way. I almost ran over the box. I drove around it, but something told me to stop and take a look."

She had to repress her anger, not at Scott but at the culprits. How could anyone do that? It was winter, and yes maybe the dogs had a thick coat of fur but that was no excuse. It was *cruel.*

She refocused her thoughts. "So, we have some more recruits for our new enterprise."

He bit his lip. "Looks that way. Sorry."

"Don't be. Just makes me even more determined to get this right."

Lucy and Scott played with the dogs a little, before taking them out for a walk and run around the woods before darkness fell.

It gave her a chance to really get to know them.

ET was the most excitable. Lou Lou sniffed around a lot; Lucy could tell she wanted to be out on the hunt.

She was otherwise content, but she wasn't going to be happy being trapped behind a fence for long. She needed more space and attention.

Berry was perfectly happy though. He had space, shelter, the open woods and two very familiar faces. Plus, he was getting all the food he wanted. He was in heaven.

The abandoned Akitas were a different story. Their fur was dirty and they were thin; clear signs of neglect.

A few more days with good food and some loving care and attention would perk them right back up though.

Now Lucy picked up one of the little furballs. "Does this guy have a name?" she asked Scott, as she cradled the pup who wriggled about as she scratched his stomach.

"I haven't had a chance to name them yet. I figure whoever gets them might want to do so themselves."

"Good point." Lucy nodded determinedly. "OK, let's get you guys all prepped and ready for a brand new life."

CHAPTER 16

*T*hey returned to the house; Lucy more eager than ever to get started on working to match all these great dogs with the perfect person.

"What do you think about this?" she asked Scott, a little while later, reciting the profile she'd just created.

She cleared her throat.

"Single, rambunctious three-year-old Kelpie named ET, phoning home. Gentle, peaceable and hard-working. He loves long walks, exercise, chasing balls, discs and playing hide-and-seek. Needs love from someone who is active and involved, and who wants a dog to put to work. Give him a job and he'll give you more than enough love in return."

"Sounds great!" Scott replied, shaking his head in admiration. "I knew you'd be amazing at this."

She smiled, thrilled with the praise. "I'll get right to work on one for Lou Lou."

"Can I make you something?" he asked as he stepped away from the table. "I haven't eaten all day."

She looked distractedly up from her notebook.

"You know, neither have I. Not since lunch anyway. That'd be nice. Thanks."

"You really are doing a great job *and* you're a natural," he commented as he walked over to the cupboards and began to collect items to prepare something.

Lucy wasn't used to hearing so much praise and she wasn't sure how to respond to it. She never did anything for recognition really; it was always passion that drove her.

And this time she had a dual reason. She wanted to help the dogs first and foremost, but helping Scott was also very satisfying. He worked hard. He cared. He wanted to do right by these animals, and she was going to see to it that he got his wish.

"I hope you like French food," he said as he began to chop some vegetables.

"Never had it," she confessed.

"Never?"

She shook her head. "I don't really go out much."

"None of your boyfriends ever took you to a French restaurant? That's a travesty."

Lucy began to fidget. "Umm, well, I never really had that many boyfriends."

"How many have you had?" he asked casually.

She hesitated. What would he think if she told him?

"I don't know if I should answer that."

"Why not? It's just a number."

74

"Fine. If it's just a number, how many girlfriends have you had?" she retorted.

"Three," he replied nonchalantly.

"That's all?" Lucy was surprised.

He smirked. "Yup. I was fifteen when I started out with Linda. We were together for three years. Broke up because of college. Susan and I got together in my junior year of college and were together for six. Then I met Hailey when I was twenty-six or seven and we were together for five. I've been single ever since."

Lucy blinked. She realized she didn't even know how old Scott was. "How old are you?"

"Thirty-three. Why?"

"Nothing," she said with a shake of her head. "Was just asking."

"So I answered your question. Now answer mine."

Discomfited, Lucy took a deep breath and sighed. "One."

"Really? Only one?"

She could hear the disbelief in his voice. "Yep. Just one."

"That's strange. I would've thought you'd be fighting them off," he stated as he continued to chop.

"Why would you think that?" she asked honestly.

"Why wouldn't I?"

Where did he get those eyes from? Whenever Lucy looked directly into them her stomach flipped about, her mind boggled and her tongue got twisted.

He was so much easier to talk to when he wasn't looking right at her.

He wouldn't be single for very long though. She could think of at least three women she knew who would be perfect for him. Tall, beautiful, intelligent and who could actually hold a conversation while making eye-to-eye contact.

"Well?" he urged.

"Well, what?" she replied, colouring.

He turned back to what he was doing. "So why haven't you dated more?"

Lucy leaned forward on her elbows and clasped her hands under her chin. "I've always been … shy," she admitted. "Painfully so, sometimes. Doesn't work well when trying to communicate with other people. Especially guys."

"You're shy?" He seemed surprised. "I wouldn't have thought so. You're so happy and chatty in my eyes."

"That's because of the dogs," she admitted. "I'm better with them than people. They don't disappoint."

"Ah OK. So, someone disappointed you," he stated perceptively.

"I guess you could say that. My dad walked out on my mom when I was eleven. She died a year later and I got sent to live with my Grandma."

Scott stopped to look back at her again. "I'm sorry to hear that."

"It's okay. It was a long time ago." She sighed. "I started seeing a guy when I was eighteen, but he was just playing with me. I thought he was serious. I guess I didn't know any better at the time."

"He was an idiot," Scott said with feeling. "Anyone

who wouldn't take someone like you seriously could only be one."

When she looked up, he was still watching her, those eyes boring into her gaze.

But this time Lucy didn't blush. She simply smiled. "Thank you."

CHAPTER 17

*V*isitors from all around the area flocked to Whitedale for this year's Holiday Fair and tree lighting ceremony.

Grant Square was the center of Whitedale; a large roundabout with a grassy middle, it was the heart of the town. And at Christmas, it was the yuletide epicenter.

White and colored strings of twinkling lights criss-crossed the square from one corner to another. Large wreaths decorated with white lights, red ribbon, and pinecones hung at the entrance from every access point.

The tree itself, erected at the center and surrounded by decorative gift boxes, was the final touch.

The official lighting ceremony occurred exactly one week before Christmas every year. Twelve feet of Douglas Fir stood fully adorned in silver, white and royal blue.

There were ribbons, balls, icicles, and the remnants of

snowfall from the night before. Even without the lights, it was beautiful.

This evening, the entire town was out in force, and Lucy was loving the holiday atmosphere.

For her 12 Dogs of Christmas matchmaking booth, Mary had given her a spot close to the Christmas tree to maximize foot traffic.

Now, standing at the booth surrounded by festive profile photos and cute bios for the dogs, it was the first time since her grandmother's death that she remembered being happy at this time of year.

"Hey Lucy," Mary called out, as she approached her with a smile. "Merry Christmas."

"Same to you. Great turnout," she commented.

The other woman looked gleeful. "Isn't it? I think it's the best we've had since I became head of the committee."

"You're doing a great job," Lucy stated as she rearranged some of the profiles out front.

Mary smiled at the presentation. "This looks great. How has the response been so far?"

Lucy beamed. It was like the sun was inside of her trying to get out. "Amazing actually," she told her. "I already have a dozen or so prospective families. I'll vet them over the next few days and hopefully have these pups cosy in their new homes in time for Christmas."

She couldn't believe the response already. So many potential families! She was sure that among them was the perfect home for each of her and Scott's furry friends.

"Keep it up," Mary encouraged. "I've got to go. It's almost showtime."

"Hey there," Scott called out then, approaching.

"You brought them!" Lucy exclaimed happily, realizing he had Lou Lou, ET, and Berry with him; their tails wagging merrily when they saw her.

"I couldn't leave these guys home, especially today. The perfect real-life canine additions."

He got closer and smiled at the display. "Wow, you did a great job with this. It looks spectacular." He picked up the flier for Rex and Roza, a couple of Border Collies he'd found in Gafferton. Their owner didn't want them and was going to put them down if no one took them, so Scott did.

"Tenacious twins Rex and Roza, six-month-old Border Collies, are looking for an active owner," he read aloud. "Energetic, intelligent, agile and balanced; they need a home where they can have lots to do. Perfect for farmers and an ideal work dog, these pooches love a cuddle after the workday is done. Both means double the love."

Lucy smiled. "Like it?"

He grinned. "It's perfect. Did you have any takers?"

Lucy grabbed the sign-up sheet and held it out to him in giddy triumph. "Four already for these two alone."

"I knew you could do it," he encouraged, as the dogs milled around, sniffing the foreign scents filling the square.

"I haven't done it *yet*," she reminded him, trying to

rein in both their enthusiasm. But she couldn't deny she was very hopeful.

"You will. I'm sure of it." Scott smiled. "Have you had a chance to look around the other stalls yet?"

"Not really. It's been so busy already. Oh hello, big guy," Berry came up to her, his huge tale almost levelling the booth, and she reached down and scratched him round the ears.

Lucy was so completely dedicated to her task that she sometimes got tunnel vision. Today was one such occasion. She really wanted to find these animals a home and that had been her foremost thought. Especially when it came to Berry.

She'd already talked to some people who were potentially great matches and hoped his new owner was amongst them. She also hoped it would be someone in, or close to town so that she could keep walking him.

She'd miss him if he wound up in a different county where she couldn't see him anymore. She couldn't be selfish, however. If the perfect home for Berry was far away, then she'd have no choice but to say goodbye.

"Well, why don't we grab a quick bite and take a look around before the ceremony starts?"

Now, Lucy looked at the big, happy dog as he wandered around the area, glancing curiously at the lights and festivity.

No, she couldn't imagine not seeing him every day. It would be a hard thing to get used to.

"Lucy?"

Her eyes snapped up at the sound of Scott's voice, and

she realized she hadn't replied. "Sorry. Yes, good idea. I was just thinking."

"About Berry?"

She nodded. "I just realized that I'm really going to miss him."

He looked at her thoughtfully. "I think maybe you should cross that bridge when you come to it."

"You're right. No sense crying over spilt milk when the carton's still in the fridge."

Scott chuckled. "A ... different take on it but yes, I guess."

"I'm a bit corny," she admitted, embarrassed. "My Grandma always said if it was something out of the way and a little bit odd, I'd probably say it."

"I think I would've very much liked to have met your grandmother," Scott stated and she smiled, realizing that Grandma in turn would have liked him a lot too.

Now he held out his arm to her. "Shall we?"

She smiled hooking it. "Let's."

CHAPTER 18

The lighting ceremony was spectacular.

The children's choir sang *Silent Night* beautifully, before Mary made her introduction to the Mayor, who duly flipped the switch and lit up the massive fir in beautiful, twinkling splendour.

Lucy and Scott watched it all as they stood side-by-side with steaming hot chocolate in hand, the dogs between them.

Scott lingered on at the booth a little after the ceremony, and when the time came for the fair to close, he stepped behind the scenes to help tidy-up, settling the dogs by a lamppost nearby.

Lucy smiled at his gallantry. "Thanks."

"My pleasure." He began to collect the fliers and place them into one of the boxes she had stored underneath the countertop.

"You know, Berry seems to like it a lot at your house," she commented, as she cleaned up. "And tonight, he behaved like a dream in your presence. Have you ever thought of taking him in yourself?"

Scott paused a little, and all of a sudden Lucy worried that she'd overstepped.

He sighed. "Berry is a great dog. We both know that. I just think that maybe there's someone else out there who'd be a better person for him."

"Really, who?" she asked, intrigued. If Scott had an idea of someone in particular then she wanted to know.

He smiled a little. "I can't say yet. I just know that I'm not the right one, sorry." He stepped closer then, and Lucy's stomach fluttered as he gently brushed a stray tendril of hair behind her ear, as if by way of apology.

She sighed and bent down to pick up a box, now feeling bad to have assumed.

"You're right, I was just reaching, and I met some really good prospects today already. It's just … I don't want to have to send him away."

"I know. But when the time comes, I know you'll do what's best for him. So, all done?" he asked as he stacked up the final box.

"I think so." All of a sudden she felt exhausted. "Man, I'm beat."

"You're like me," Scott chuckled. "Once I get my teeth into something I can't stop until it's done. I'll skip meals and even showers."

Her face wrinkled. "That's gross."

"No, that's manual labour. When I want to get work done on the house I get up, put on some clothes and get to it. I can shower before bed. I just need to get going."

"I hope you don't plan to do that when you find your next girlfriend," she commented. "I'm sure she wouldn't find you nearly as appealing."

"Trust me, if I had a girlfriend, there would be a lot of different things in my life."

She turned to look at him, wondering what he meant. What would he even need to change?

"So - see you tomorrow?" Scott enquired, as he closed the door of Lucy's truck once they'd got everything back inside.

"I could maybe stop by after I finish following up with some of the families. We could discuss the options? I've got a lot to get through over the next few days."

"Great. I can make you dinner and you can see Berry of course," he added with a grin.

"Sounds great to me. See you then," Lucy turned her key in the ignition, and glanced back at the twinkling Christmas tree, the backdrop to a waving Scott and his waggy-tailed companions.

And as she drove away, she couldn't help but smile.

Despite her tiredness, tonight had been the nicest time she'd spent in ages.

CHAPTER 19

*D*ays passed and Lucy went about her dog-walking duties as normal, but as soon as she dropped her charges back, off she went to visit prospective owners for the rescues.

The very first day, she found a home for two of the Akita puppies and was over the moon when she went to Scott's that evening to share the news and see Berry.

Day after day, the process went pretty much the same. She walked her dogs as usual, then afterwards visited prospective owners before meeting up with Scott and Berry.

Some days she had good news to share and others, she just went to see Berry, enjoy Scott's company - and not have to go home to an empty apartment.

"I think ET's going to be so happy," she told Scott now, excited to have found a match for his rescue pup. "Joseph Steinbeck is perfect for him. He's a fireman and trains every day, so taking ET for walks and getting him exercise won't be a problem. Plus, he said they're looking at adding more dogs to the rescue team and ET would be ideal for that. Yes, he's a bit on the older side to start training, but from what I've observed he's very compliant and with the right trainer and some patience, could make a great rescue dog."

"You're really excited about this," Scott mused as he brought a platter of pizza over to the couch.

Drinks were already on the coffee table and Lucy was curled up on the couch with the remote in her hand surfing Netflix for a movie.

"Aren't you?"

"Of course. And I knew you'd be great at all this, I just never thought it would all happen so quickly. You know, I think we truly are going to get all these guys re-homed in time for Christmas."

"Of course we are," Lucy said satisfied. "Once I make a plan I execute it."

"Good to know."

Scott settled on the couch beside her. Lucy wasn't sure what she was in the mood to watch tonight. TV could be a wasteland; you could get lost and never actually find that one thing you wanted to watch. It was the ultimate 'too much choice' dilemma.

"Having trouble deciding?" he asked as she continued to skim through titles.

"I don't know what I feel like tonight," she admitted. "You pick."

He took the remote from her as Lucy pulled out a

slice of meat lover's pizza. Scott had doubled every topping, making it the most loaded pizza she'd ever seen.

When she looked back at the screen, she laughed out loud at the title he'd highlighted.

"OK. *Lassie* it is."

CHAPTER 20

*I*t was now only three days til Christmas and Lucy was still on the hunt for a home for Berry.

Lou Lou, ET and the Akitas were gone. A farmer named Jasper Tucker had taken Lou Lou. He liked to go on frequent hunting trips, was in his thirties and active. He was perfect for a Coonhound.

Now, she was personally delivering Rex and Roza to their new owners.

"Now, dogs are fun, but a really big responsibility," she informed the Dickersons' two small children.

"Can I ride on their backs?" four-year-old Billy asked. "I saw it on TV."

Lucy smiled indulgently. "That's actually not so good for the dogs. They weren't built to bear weight on their backs like that. You could hurt them."

"Then why did they do it on TV?" Five-year-old Sydney wanted to know.

Their parents smiled. "They're just curious," their mother commented.

"That's good, means they're interested," Lucy replied. She turned back to the children. "They probably didn't know better, but you do now, so you can take even better care of your new furry friends. That's what you want, right?"

The children chorused a happy yes.

"Now Rex and Roza aren't like your toys, OK? You have to help your mom and dad take care of them." The children were too young to take care of the dogs on their own, but it was good to have them help so that one day they could take more responsibility.

Good pet ownership started when kids were small, Lucy believed. Not that she thought they'd have any trouble here. The Dickersons owned a ranch, and animals were everywhere.

Rex and Roza would have work to do once they were older, but for now, they were a great addition to the family.

Lucy left the children to play with their new pets while she turned her focus to the ones who'd really be taking care of the dogs, their parents.

"So I know we went through everything before, but I just wanted to emphasize a few things. When it comes to their diet, make sure you watch them carefully. They do a lot of exercising, but you have to be wary of overfeeding them. Treats will help you to train them, but too many can affect their weight. Here are a few."

She handed over the bag of treats she usually bought

for her charges. "You'll want to use a pin brush once or twice a week to keep their coat free of mats, tangles, and debris. You'll need to do that more frequently during shedding season."

"Shedding season?" Lynda Dickerson asked.

"Yes. It gets pretty hairy then," Lucy mused ruefully. "But you'll be fine. You're just going to need to brush them more. You can make it something fun for the kids to do. Speaking of the children … collies tend to want to lead those smaller than them, animals and children. Your two are a bit older, and you've said they're well-behaved so that shouldn't be a problem, but I'd still keep an eye on them just for the initial phase, as both the kids and the dogs adjust."

"Thank you," James said. "We've had dogs before but we've never had anyone do what you've done in making sure we got the right animals for our family, and our family's needs. Plus, you seem to care about the well-being of these animals. There should be more like you."

Lucy could feel her cheeks getting hot with the compliment. She wasn't used to them and it only made her social discomfort even more apparent.

Still, she couldn't deny that all of this was making her feel good.

"Thank you."

BUT AT THIS POINT, everyone had a home but Berry.

Lucy had met with several families who were interested in having the big dog as an addition to their family.

95

They'd made it onto her list, so they had the basic requirements, but once she met them, she saw the faults.

"I'm sorry Mr. Chase, I just don't think Berry would fit here," Lucy stated as she sat in the living room of Simon Chase's house.

"Why not?" he asked. "I have space outside and I can afford the cost of his care."

"Yes, that's true," she replied. "But he doesn't like staying outside all the time. His previous owner, Mrs. Cole, kept him exclusively in the house at night. Your house is a great size, but you have a lot of stuff in here and I can tell some of it is expensive. Outside just wouldn't work with Berry. He likes to be where the family is and he can't do that in here."

Simon nodded. "It wouldn't matter to me much. I'm sure I could get it done. Maybe move a few things around?"

"You could try, but it might just make you and Berry uncomfortable. Truthfully, I think another type of dog would suit you best."

"I see. Thank you for your honesty," Simon said as he extended his hand to her.

"I'm really sorry to disappoint you," she continued as she got to her feet and took his hand.

"It's quite alright. Thanks for coming out."

But as Lucy left yet another fruitless prospective match for Berry, she had to wonder if maybe the ultimate fault lay with her.

CHAPTER 21

She ambled back to her truck, unable to shake the thought.

Simon Chase would've been a great match for Berry, albeit not for the inside of his house.

What was she saying? She could've let it slide and let him have Berry. Did it matter that he wouldn't be living the same way he did with Mrs. Cole? He was out of the house a lot with Scott now as it was.

And if Simon Chase was willing to risk his property, who was she to say otherwise?

"You have to stop being so particular," she told herself as she got back into the vehicle. She sat behind the wheel and stared out at the slowly falling snow.

Berry was special to her though. She wanted him to have the perfect situation.

OK, so her apartment was small, and her landlord wouldn't let her have a dog, but Lucy couldn't help but think that he still would've been happiest of all with her.

She certainly would've felt better. She wouldn't need to worry about him. She could take care of him just the way Mrs Cole would've wanted.

She could do it.

So maybe she should think about getting a different apartment?

It could work, she realized excitedly. She could look for someplace else to live. Someplace big enough for her and Berry, with a landlord who didn't mind pets.

Lucy started the truck. She'd bounce the idea off Scott and see what he thought.

"I THINK IT'S ME," she sighed when later, she flopped down at a chair around Scott's makeshift kitchen table.

"What is?" he asked, as poured kibble into a bowl for Berry.

"Not being able to find a home for this big guy. Maybe I'm too picky."

"Not necessarily. You just know Berry so well and who'd be right for him. Look what you did for my rescues. Every last one of them has the perfect home now, and that was all you."

"So why not Berry then? Why is it so hard?"

"I don't know," he said. "Why don't you tell me?"

"I was thinking about it while I was leaving the Chase house. Maybe I keep finding faults in every prospective pet owner, because deep down inside I don't believe anyone would take care of Berry as well as I would," she admitted.

Scott turned to her with raised eyebrows. "Keep going."

"You aren't going to say anything?"

"Not right now. I'd rather hear where else you're going with this."

"Well," she said, continuing. "I know I don't have the perfect place to keep him right now. My apartment is small, but I could change that. I could get a new place. It might take a while, but I could do it."

"What would you do with him until then?"

She grimaced a little. "I was kinda hoping I could leave him here with you if you'd let me?" she asked hopefully. "It wouldn't be for long. I hope. Just until I found a bigger place that would suit both of us."

"A different apartment?"

"No other choice. Besides, it's not as though he'd be home alone when I'm working because I'd take him on all the walks with me as normal."

"True."

Scott put the dog food away and handed Lucy the bowl. They walked to the holding area together where Berry was running around the enclosure and came bounding up to the gate the second he saw them.

Lucy smiled, she would never get tired of the sight of him running towards her, his large ears flopping on either side of his head, tongue hanging out as if he was smiling.

They opened the gate and stepped inside. Lucy walked to the kennel, but Berry was already trying to get his head into the bowl.

"Hold on a minute," she giggled as she gently pushed his head away and set the food down. Berry bounded over and dove right in the second she stepped away.

She stood staring at the big dog with her hands stuffed in her pockets, then looked at Scott. "I'm being silly, aren't I?"

"Why would you say that?" he asked.

"To think I could honestly do a better job taking care of him than people who have the space and are willing to compromise their lifestyle to have him." She sighed heavily.

Scott's hand moved to rest gently on her shoulder. "I don't think so."

Lucy turned to look at him, surprised. "Really?"

"Really."

"So you think this could be the right thing?" she asked, hopeful.

"I think you've finally realized what I've known all along," he said gently and turned her to face him. His hands were on her arms, holding her gently. "Lucy, you *are* his perfect person."

She couldn't describe what it felt like when she heard those words come out of Scott's mouth. Deep down inside she'd always known she didn't want a dog *like* Berry. She wanted *him*. She wanted the big guy as her pet, her trusty companion, but was content to just help Mrs Cole.

Then, the more time she got to spend with him, the more she realized how great it was to have him with her all the time.

"Thanks for that," she told Scott as she smiled up at him.

"For what?"

"For saying that. I needed to hear it."

"Why?"

"I guess I needed to know someone else besides me thought it was a good fit," she admitted bashfully. "I may not have everything he needs right now, but ..." She shrugged.

"I agree. Sometimes you don't have to have everything perfect though, Lucy. Sometimes you just have to have the heart. That's enough for now. The rest will come. And you have the heart," he continued. "I've known that for ages. It's why I wanted to meet you."

His confession took her by surprise. "You - meet me?

"Yes. Mrs. Cole told me about this wonderful woman who came to walk Berry," he chuckled. "She raved about you."

The sentiment made Lucy's heart sing. She'd never told Mrs Cole how highly she regarded her, so it was nice to know that the older woman felt the same way about her.

"That day we met was purely coincidental, but the second I saw you running behind Berry, I knew you were the best person for both of them," Scott continued. "Mrs. Cole needed someone to help, and Berry needed someone who could give him what she no longer could."

Lucy was beaming now.

"Since then I've watched you go all out for him. Persuading people to take care of him. Trying to find a home day after day. You were relentless, and the person who loved him enough to do all of that could only be the best one for him." He looked directly at her, those eyes boring into her gaze again. "You're the perfect match, Lucy. I've just been waiting for you to realize it."

CHAPTER 22

*L*ucy hadn't really been able to enjoy Christmas since her grandmother's death.

But this would be the first time in years that she wasn't going to spend the day alone.

Instead, Scott had asked her over. She brought a homemade pecan pie with her and a bottle of mulled wine that she'd bought at the fair.

He was waiting on the porch when she arrived; Berry beside him. The big dog ran to her the second she got out of the truck and immediately tried to stick his big head in the pie.

"Oh no you don't," she chided gently. "This isn't for you."

The dog snorted and walked away.

"For the first time, I think you disappointed him," Scott commented as he leaned against the post watching her. She had a red wool hat on her head and a cosy matching peacoat.

The snow that morning was heavy and the wind icy in every direction.

"Aren't you cold?" she asked him as she approached the entryway. Though he was wearing a cosy sweater that looked like it could be cashmere.

Having only ever seen him in work shirts and jeans, it was a nice change.

"I have the heating on," he said with a smile. "Besides, I wasn't out here long. Berry let me know you were on your way."

"He must've heard the truck coming down the road," Lucy mused as she stepped inside.

However, the sound of another vehicle approaching from behind drew her attention and she turned back to see two cars and another truck making their way up the driveway. "Who's that?" she asked a little unnerved.

"Just a few of my friends," Scott said casually.

"Your friends?" Lucy almost shrieked. She'd come over today thinking it was just the two of them, a casual thing as always. She wasn't ready to meet strangers.

"Don't be scared," he chuckled, reading her mind. "They won't bite. I promise."

"Why didn't you tell me though?"

"I didn't know they were coming until this morning. They wanted to surprise me and drove all the way here from Denver. I couldn't tell them no." He gave her a big smile and then took the pie from her hands. Why did he have to smile like that? It made Lucy forget about her shyness. "Besides, I wanted them to meet you," he added mysteriously.

"Me ...why?"

"Is there something wrong with wanting my oldest friends to meet one of my newest?" he responded.

"What if they don't like me? You know I'm not great with strangers."

"Who is?" He shook his head. "It doesn't matter anyway. I've already told them all about you."

Lucy's eyes widened. "What did you tell them?"

"Just that I met this crazy woman who loves dogs and smiles like sunshine," he commented offhandedly.

Her heart fluttered, but she dismissed it with a scoff.

"So you made me sound way better than I am."

"I don't exaggerate, Lucy. If I say you're wonderful, it's because you are."

Then, before she could react, Scott winked and hopped down off the porch to greet his friends.

CHAPTER 23

"*M*erry Christmas!" a cheerful female voice called out.

It belonged to a lithe blonde. She ran to Scott, threw her arms around his neck and smacked his cheek with a kiss. "You big lug. How've you been?" But didn't give him a chance to reply before she turned to Lucy. "And you must be Lucy. So nice to meet you finally," she said moving to embrace her too.

Finally...? Lucy was completely off-guard but did her best to return the welcoming gesture.

"Ted, could you get those things in here pronto?" the woman asked, turning to a man getting stuff out of the car behind her. "Kids, come on in out of the cold." She looked to Scott again. "Where's the bathroom these days?"

"Through there, just past the kitchen," he indicated with a roll of his eyes. "Same as last time."

"I'll drop this off on the way," She grabbed the pie from Scott's hands and hurried on her way.

Lucy watched her go. "Who was that?" she laughed.

"That whirlwind is Roxanna. I've known her since I was in high school. She's a bundle of energy and the friendliest person you'll ever meet."

"Uncle Scott!" a chorus sounded as three children, two girls and a boy came running in their direction.

"Hey, here comes trouble!" Scott declared as he stooped to hug them.

"We missed you, Uncle Scott," said the oldest girl. She was blonde like her mother and cute as a button.

"Me or my hot chocolate?"

"The chocolate," they answered in unison, and Lucy had to smile.

"At least you're honest," Scott turned to introduce her. "This is Lucy. And this is Jennifer, Morgan, and Tyler."

"Hi!" they all chorused together. They were adorable and he was adorable with them.

"Hey kids," she answered with a small wave. "Merry Christmas."

"Get inside and take your jackets off. The TV's that way," he added and they scampered off immediately.

"And this is Roxy's husband Ted," Scott supplied, as a tall, slightly balding man approached the house.

"Don't tell me. Lucy," he commented with a smile. "I'd give you a hug but as you can see I'm the bag man for this trip."

She laughed. "Would you like some help?"

"Love some to be honest."

"I can get it," Scott interjected.

"No, you have more guests to greet. I can help," Lucy insisted as she grabbed a few of the packages Ted had in his arms.

Soon the other guests arrived. Anita and Paul, two of Scott's friends from Ireland who were staying with Bryan and his sister Lydia in Denver, had chosen to tag along when they heard of their impromptu plan to surprise him.

They had come prepared too. They brought turkey and stuffing, sweet potato pie, macaroni and cheese, salads, garlic bread, and wine.

Along with the roast ham, potatoes, candied yams, green beans and pumpkin soup Scott had already prepared, they had a true Christmas feast to look forward to.

THE FOOD LASTED ALL the way through the afternoon, with Ted then whipping out some beers.

The men set up in front of the TV, while the women chatted in the kitchen and the kids preoccupied themselves with the gifts their parents had brought, but mostly with Berry.

The big dog was a huge hit amongst the guests.

They each took turns scratching behind his ears and commenting on how amicable he was, surprised that a dog that big could be so gentle and easy with children.

"So Lucy, we've all heard tons about you, and now that it's just us girls here," Roxy grinned, indicating the guys who were enthralled in a game on TV. "What's the deal with you two?"

She looked up in slight alarm. "Me and Scott?"

"Yes," the other woman pressed. "Spill."

They were standing around the kitchen island staring at her, as Lydia washed the dishes and Lucy dried.

Roxy was responsible for packing them away.

"Oh yes, do tell," Lydia urged. "We promise not to say a word." She grinned and continued to scrub the remnants of the turkey roast from the pan.

"Well, Scott's my friend obviously. He's … nice," Lucy replied nervously.

She hated being put on the spot at the best of times, but this was even worse. They were questioning her relationship with Scott and she wasn't entirely sure what that was. They'd become so close this last while, but that was it. Wasn't it?

"That's it?" Anita scoffed. "Please, anyone can tell that guy is falling *hard*."

"You think so?" Lucy questioned uncertainly.

"Definitely," Roxy agreed. "When a guy talks about a woman as much as he talks about you, there has to be more to it than he's saying."

"So he said something to you?"

"Of course not," Lydia replied with a roll of her eyes. "He denies there's anything, just like you're doing," she grinned. "Thing is I don't believe either of you."

"Don't believe what?" Scott's voice interjected suddenly.

"That there's nothing between you and Lucy, that's what," Roxy stated.

"What's between him and Lucy?" Bryan asked, going to the fridge for another beer.

Scott looked at Lucy and she looked back at him, her cheeks reddening.

"See, look at them," Roxy reiterated. "Why don't you two stop playing coy and just admit it?"

"Rox …" her husband warned.

Scott cleared his throat. "If there was something to say…"

"… then we would," Lucy put in quickly.

Lydia chuckled. "They're even finishing each other's sentences already."

"Definitely something there," Bryan teased.

"Why are you all so eager to make Lucy and me into something?" Scott asked nonchalantly.

"Because it's painfully obvious there *is* something," Roxanna tut-tutted. "We'd all like to see you happy, and I'm sure I speak for everyone when I say that from what we've heard and seen today, we all give you two a big thumbs up."

Despite herself, Lucy smiled brightly. "You guys are great too," she said.

"See! Perfect! She fits naturally into our ragtag bunch," Roxanna continued as she draped an arm around Lucy's neck. She looked at Scott. "So why not just come right out and say it?"

"Rox, if I had something to say, I assure you it would

not be public," Scott replied firmly. "And when I do have something to say, Lucy will be the first to hear it."

His gaze met hers as she spoke and she found her breath catch in her lungs. This was incredibly … awkward.

What did he mean?

"Forgive my wife," Ted demurred, as he came over and hugged Roxanna from behind. "Once she gets something into her head, she doesn't let go."

"Got that right. That's how I snagged you." Roxanna planted a light kiss on his lips, and they all laughed.

"Way to change the subject," Bryan commented with a chuckle. "Now is there any more beer …"

CHAPTER 24

$\mathcal{I}$t was after eight that evening when the group decided that it was time to leave. It was starting to snow again, and they needed to get going if they wanted to make it back to the city before the worst of it.

Lucy and Scott stood on the porch and waved good-bye. He draped his arm lightly around her shoulders and she leaned against him as the snow fell gently all around.

It was the kind of warm, cosy, *homely* holiday moment she'd only ever seen on TV.

And she couldn't believe it was real.

This Christmas had yielded more than she could ever expect. Not only did she have a new friend, but friends plural.

And lately with Scott, a real sense of companionship; something that she'd been missing for far too long.

"So, what do you think? Not a complete disaster, right?" he asked as he closed the door behind them.

"I think they're wonderful," she admitted. "I really liked them all and the kids are so sweet."

"So I hope you're not going to leave me now too?" he asked, as he turned to her.

The cars were almost out of sight.

She shook her head. She'd just had the nicest Christmas Day ever and she didn't want it to end just yet. "Why do good things always go by so quickly though?"

"So we can have more of them," Scott shivered. "Let's get back inside out of this cold. Feel like some hot chocolate?" he suggested, leading back inside.

"I'd love some. Though I truly didn't think I could fit in anything else after all that food."

The kitchen was immaculate now, with little to no remnants of the humongous feast that had been enjoyed earlier that day.

"Go find a movie. I'll bring the chocolate," Scott stated as he began pulling out ingredients.

Lucy wandered into the living room.

Berry was nestled by the fireplace snoozing contentedly, and she had to smile.

Like it or not, the big dog had pretty much already made this house his home.

Scott came in a few minutes later with two steaming cups of his famous homemade hot chocolate. His was plain but there were marshmallows on hers, just as she liked it.

He stretched out on the couch and Lucy adjusted herself on the opposite end, with her feet towards him.

"*It's a Wonderful Life* is on. Do you want to watch it?" It was her all-time favourite Christmas movie. She could never get over James Stewart's characterization of George Bailey.

Scott smiled. "I love that movie. My Mom liked to watch it every Christmas," he informed her.

They settled down to watch the movie, while the fire crackled lightly beneath the TV screen, Berry asleep beneath it.

Lucy sipped at the warm beverage, feeling more content and cosy than she'd ever been in her entire life.

Scott tugged at her toes and she giggled.

"Merry Christmas Lucy."

She smiled. "Merry Christmas."

THEY MUST'VE FALLEN asleep watching the movie because when Lucy was awakened by Berry's damp tongue licking her face, the sun was just coming up over the horizon.

Across the way, Scott was still asleep, now hugging a cushion to his chest.

She couldn't help but watch him as he slept so peacefully, properly studying the contours of his face without having to worry about him catching her.

Berry nudged her again.

"Alright, I get it. You're hungry," she whispered.

She eased herself from the couch and padded into the kitchen. She got his bowl and the dog food and fixed him his breakfast.

Then she had an idea. Scott had cooked for her so

many times already; why didn't she do something for him today?

Lucy set to work at making breakfast. She knew where most things were, having watched him prepare stuff for her so many times.

Soon, she had everything she needed to make them something delicious.

He kept a well-stocked pantry and everything was there to make sweet crepes, sausages, eggs and biscuits.

It had been a while since she'd had a reason to make a big meal like this, and wouldn't bother for just herself, but for Scott, it was no trouble.

The smell must have awakened him because he walked into the room just as Lucy was plating the eggs.

"Morning," she greeted cheerfully.

"Good morning," he replied with a grin. "What's all this?"

"This is what I like to call breakfast," she replied. "Have a seat." She brought the plates and cutlery to the table, along with the pot of coffee she'd brewed. "Bon appétit."

They talked and laughed and ate. She couldn't remember ever feeling so at ease with anyone.

Scott was special, that was clear, but the problem was the more Lucy spent time with him and the more they shared, the more she realized she wanted.

CHAPTER 25

*S*cott cleaned up after, protesting that the cook didn't clean where he was from.

Lucy appreciated the sentiment, but she was happy to do it, after all, it was his house and she'd made the mess.

But he wasn't hearing of it.

Berry began to bark at the door. He'd been pacing back and forth for a few minutes.

"I think he wants a walk," Lucy said.

"Let's take him then. I'll get our jackets."

He returned a few minutes later with both of their jackets and helped her slip hers on.

Berry was already gone, bounding off into the woods ahead of them.

She laughed as she watched the big happy dog running around in the snow chasing his tail.

"Look at him," she said with a chuckle. "He just loves it here."

"He does. It's really good having him here too," Scott replied. "How do you like it?"

"What're you talking about? You know I *love* this place. It's amazing," Lucy gasped. "The kind of house anyone would be excited to come home to."

"That's why I chose this spot. I used to love coming here to fish as a kid, so when I heard that it was up for sale I had to grab it."

"Good thing. If I could afford a place like this I would too. It's perfect for dogs and for relaxing in nature. The human company isn't so bad either," she teased with a smile.

"I could say the same about you."

Scott was looking directly at her now, and Lucy's heart was beating faster. "Your friends seem to think there's something more," she said boldly, surprising herself by being so direct.

But she needed to know.

"Do you think there is?" he asked, as they ambled out onto the wooden pier.

The sun was now peeking up just over the mountains.

"I don't know. Is there?" Lucy's heart was beating so fast, she didn't know how she got the words out.

She caught sight of Berry out of the corner of her eye and her heart steadied again as it always did.

He was occupied looking down at his reflection. He loved to look at himself. Mirrors, water, you name it. The big guy loved his own image.

"What do *you* think?" Scott repeated, still not answering her question.

His eyes were still locked on her face.

Lucy sucked in a breath. It was now or never.

"There is for me. What I want to know is -"

She didn't get to finish her sentence. The second the words left her mouth Scott had closed the space between them.

It was so quick that Lucy hadn't a chance to think about what to do before his lips pressed against hers, and her body was pulled flush against him.

Thankfully, she didn't need to think.

What she was feeling was enough. Her senses were reeling, but her fingers still worked. They curled into the lapels of Scott's jacket and held him. It wasn't enough though. A moment later her hands slipped up from his chest and encircled his neck.

His lips moved over hers like silk over skin.

When they finally parted, she was breathless. It took her several seconds to open her eyes. She didn't want to break the spell she was under, but she had to. She had to look at him.

"I've wanted to do that for a long time," he confessed. "I was waiting."

"I'm glad you didn't wait any longer." She chuckled. "I guess Roxy was right."

Scott laughed. "She's always right."

"I'm glad," Lucy stepped toward him again. She raised her chin and pressed her lips to his lightly. "I think I wanted to do that for a long time too."

"Why didn't you?"

119

The fact that they were having this conversation at all, was still something Lucy was trying to process.

It was made difficult with him looking at her as if she was the most beautiful person he'd ever seen. She'd only ever seen that look in movies. Never directed at her.

"I didn't realize it before," she admitted. "I thought we were just friends. The only thing between us was our love of dogs," she continued. "The jittery feeling in my stomach whenever I was around you was just because of my shyness, I told myself."

"But it wasn't?"

"No," she replied with a small shake of her head, amazed at her certainty and the fact that she was confident about admitting all this to him. "It was telling me what I hadn't figured out yet."

"I'm just glad we both got the same feeling."

"You know, this stuff doesn't happen to people like me," Lucy laughed softly, and tucked her hair behind her ear.

"People don't fall in love where you're from?" he teased.

Her eyes must've looked like saucers.

"What did you say?"

He smiled. "I said I've fallen in love with you Lucy Adams."

Her face lit up at the words. She could feel the heat radiating from her cheeks as she grinned at him.

CHAPTER 26

*L*ucy hadn't truly realized she'd fallen for Scott.

It was all so subtle like the mist rolling in on the surface of a lake. It crept in and before she knew it the house of her heart was filled with it. Pillar to post. Roof to basement.

"I think … I love you too," she whispered.

He reached for her hand and pulled her gently to him. She fell against him, her hands flat against his chest.

"You know, watching you blush just makes me smile because I know you aren't a woman who pretends. You call it shyness, but actually, I think it's just wearing your heart on your sleeve. I can trust that. I can trust you."

"Scott…"

"Listen. I told myself I wasn't taking another chance on a woman. I'd sworn off romance long before I met you. Even after Mrs. Cole told me about you, I just wanted to know the person who had come to mean so much to her. Then we met. The minute I saw your smile, I knew there was something about you."

She laughed. "All I thought was that you were the cutest construction worker I'd ever seen."

He laughed. "Thanks."

"I didn't think we'd see each other again after that. I was glad when we did," she admitted. "Berry coming across your house that day saved me."

"Saved us both you mean. After that, when I took Berry in and you started visiting him here, I realized that I wanted more. I wanted a relationship, someone I could come home to and drink my mother's hot chocolate with on cold evenings. Someone who would curl up with me on Christmas night by the fire, while the dog slept on the rug."

"I think we've already covered that bit," she chuckled.

"Yeah, we did, and we weren't even trying," Scott answered. "It just happened naturally, like everything else with you and me."

"And I liked coming here," she admitted after a moment. "I liked driving out here and being welcomed. I liked watching you cook," she said with a smile. "That was a surprise."

"And I like cooking for you."

"I've never felt so comfortable around a guy before," Lucy admitted. "Usually, I can't put two words together, but with you, any nervousness just sort of melted away. One second, I couldn't think straight when you were near, the next I found I didn't want to stop talking to you."

"Feeling's mutual, believe me."

Her skin felt as if a gentle electric current was moving over it. The hairs on her arms stood on end and she shivered.

"Lucy?"

"Yes?"

"I'm going to kiss you again if you don't stop me," he declared.

She smiled brightly. "So what's stopping you?"

He really was the best kisser on the planet.

Tender and warm. His hands were firm but soft against her skin. The cold wind that blew off the water was nothing. She couldn't even feel it. His kiss was dizzying, intoxicating, and she was enjoying every second of it.

Berry must've gotten tired looking at his reflection because a moment later he was back by their side with his head nuzzling at their legs.

He barked low and then trotted around them happily.

"I think he approves," Scott commented.

Lucy looked at the big dog and smiled. "I think so too."

"What do you say about us all getting back indoors and having more of my mom's special hot chocolate?"

"Do you still have marshmallows?" she asked as he took her hand and began to lead her toward the house.

"When I knew you were coming for Christmas I bought two bags when I went to the store."

"I do believe you're getting to know me."

"I look forward to knowing everything about you," Scott replied as he squeezed her hand gently. "The full profile. But we don't need one of your matchmaking cards this time. I want to take my own time."

Lucy liked the sound of that.

Berry trotted up beside them, and she let her fingers rest on his back comfortingly.

"It's nearly finished?" Lucy commented now, as she looked at the house. She hadn't seen it from this angle before, but now she could see that he'd finished the roof above the porch, and a lot more had been done to the far side of the house.

"Just about. I had a lot of motivation lately…"

"Motivation?"

"I thought maybe a certain fellow dog-lover might one day if things went well …. like to make it her home." He looked hesitantly at Lucy and squeezed her hand as they walked and she couldn't speak for joy. "Only if she wanted to of course," he added quickly. "It even comes equipped with a place for her dog."

Emotion consumed her. She'd always known this house would be the perfect home for Berry.

She'd just never expected it could be the perfect forever home for her too.

She smiled at Scott.

"Sounds to me like a match made in heaven."

CHRISTMAS BENEATH THE STARS

EXCERPT

Cosy up with another heartwarming festive romance
from the Irish Times #1 bestselling author - airing now
in the US as a Christmas movie!

CHAPTER 1

*H*annah Reid loved Christmas.

She loved the cheery feeling in the atmosphere, the twinkling, festive lights and most of all, the sense that at this magical time of the year, anything was possible.

She couldn't add frost or snow to the list though; a born and bred Californian, Hannah wasn't familiar with more traditional wintery Christmas weather.

Yet.

Andy Williams' warm vocals filled the buds in her ears as she reclined in her seat and peered out the window of the aircraft to an ocean of darkness and lights. It would be her first holiday season away from home. Her first ever white Christmas.

It was indeed the most wonderful time of the year ...

Hannah hummed the cheery festive tune and glanced down at the cover of the magazine on her lap, a broad smile spreading across her face.

It still felt like a dream.

Discover Wild, one of the biggest wildlife magazines in the country, was sending *her* - Hannah - on assignment.

She ran her hand over the cover shot of a tigress and her cub as they nuzzled together.

It was an amazing photo, one she would have killed to have taken herself.

"Soon," she mused. *Soon it could be my stuff on the cover. All I have to do is get one perfect shot and I'm on my way to a permanent gig with* Discover Wild.

She hugged the magazine to her chest and closed her eyes, relaxing back against the soft leather seat.

IT FELT LIKE JUST A MOMENT, but when Hannah woke it was to the sound of the pilot announcing their descent into Anchorage.

She sat up immediately and looked out the window.

Everything was white!

She'd never seen anything so beautiful. The mountains surrounding the airport were blanketed in thick snow, and a light dusting covered everything else.

She could see the men on the tarmac clearing away the snow, as half a dozen planes in every size - large Boeings to small Cessnas - lay waiting, along with a row of buses to the side.

She wondered which one of those would be taking her to the holiday village she'd chosen as her accommodation while here.

'Nestled deep in the Alaskan wilderness, Christmas World is a true holiday fairytale if ever there was one.

Set amidst lush forest on the South banks of the Yukon River, escape to a magical land where Santa comes to visit every year, and you can find a helpful elf around every corner. Immerse yourself in our idyllic winter paradise and enjoy a Christmas you will never forget ...'

Hannah couldn't wait to experience the true, out-and-out winter wonderland the online description promised.

Now, the flight was on the ground, but no one was moving. There was a backup of some sort, and passengers were asked to stay on the plane while it was resolved.

Hannah wasn't too bothered; they'd arrived half an hour early in any case, which meant she still had plenty of time before her transfer.

She preoccupied herself with her phone and more online information and picturesque photographs of Christmas World.

The resort homepage featured a group of happy smiling visitors, with various green-and-red-clad elves in their midst.

In the background, picture-perfect buildings akin to colourful gingerbread houses dusted with snow framed a traditional town square. It was exactly the kind of Christmas experience Hannah had always dreamed about as a child.

She couldn't *wait* to be there.

CHAPTER 2

Over an hour later, Hannah was still waiting.

In Anchorage International Airport with forty or so other travellers.

Their Christmas World transfer - the so-called 'Magical Christmas Caravan' was late ... *very* late.

"You can't be serious," a fellow airline passenger commented nearby. "How much longer are we supposed to wait? Are they going to compensate us for this debacle? It is the resort's transport after all," the disgruntled woman asked.

She was surrounded by three miserable-looking children, while her sullen husband stood in a long line of people trying to find out what was going on.

Hannah had noticed the family on the plane earlier, but now she was getting a better look at them. They were exactly the type of people you'd expect to find on such a jaunt; happy family, blonde-haired and blue-eyed, with their cute-as-a-button kids giddy with excitement about a trip of a lifetime to see Santa.

More decidedly *un*happy faces surrounded the resort's airport help desk at the moment, but there were plenty of content ones to be found elsewhere too.

A father with his son excitedly perched on top of his shoulders. A serene mother with her sleeping child, and an elderly couple holding hands while they waited for their connection.

It was everything the holidays should be about, Hannah thought; family and loved ones together at the most magical time of the year.

She had been in plenty of airports, but there was something about this one that appealed to her photographer's eye.

The nearby pillars were like pieces of art, almost abstract; though she didn't really know much about art except what she did or didn't like. These were adorned from top to bottom with garlands and white lights. While elsewhere in the terminal, festive wreaths hung on hooks and there were lots and lots of fresh-smelling pine trees.

And of course, then there was the view.…

Hannah had taken countless pictures in her life, some to pay the bills and many more for fun. She'd taken portraits, and even the occasional wedding when things were slow between wildlife jobs, but there was something about the outdoors that she loved most of all.

She'd spent her entire life in it after all, had hiked the Quarry trail in Auburn so many times she felt she knew it by heart. Same for the Recreational River, Blue Heron Trail and the Simpson-Reed Trail, and that was just California.

She'd zigzagged her way across America with her collection of trusty Nikon SLR cameras, but she'd never ventured this far north.

The furthest she'd been was Alberta for a wildlife safari last summer. It was those photos that had opened the door to her current opportunity.

And the reason she was in this snowy picture perfect wonderland right now.

AN HOUR OR SO LATER, and Hannah was peering out the window of Christmas World's transfer coach as Anchorage melted away in a sea of white.

Fresh snow had begun to fall half an hour before, which almost made up for the exorbitant wait.

But at least they were on their way now, and soon Hannah would have a warm lodge, a toasty fire and the most magical Christmas experience awaiting her.

She wondered if there really would be fresh roasted chestnuts available as advertised, and what kind of activities there would be for guests to enjoy when they arrived.

The website listed things like dog-sledding and carolling, plus places to get hot chocolate, Christmas cookies, and a myriad other festive treats.

All of which sounded amazing, especially since she

was tired and in sore need of some holiday cheer after such a long travel day.

She imagined the resort town as something like from the movie, *It's A Wonderful Life,* with that close-knit community feel throughout.

Yes, she was here primarily for a career opportunity, but she'd be lying if she said there wasn't the element of living out a fantasy white Christmas too.

Hannah turned back to the window. The snow was falling harder now, and the smile wouldn't leave her face.

She was about to have the best Christmas ever; she could feel it.

And she couldn't wait for it to begin.

It's like Christmas morning. The faster you sleep, the faster it arrives.

Isn't that what Mom and Dad always said?

End of Excerpt

CHRISTMAS BENEATH THE STARS is out now in print and ebook.

ABOUT THE AUTHOR

International #1 and USA Today bestselling author Melissa Hill lives in County Wicklow, Ireland. Her page-turning emotional stories of family, friendship and romance have been translated into 25 different languages and are regular chart-toppers internationally.

A Reese Witherspoon x Hello Sunshine adaptation of her worldwide bestseller SOMETHING FROM TIFFANY'S is airing now on Amazon Prime Video worldwide.

THE CHARM BRACELET aired in 2020 as a holiday movie 'A Little Christmas Charm'. A GIFT TO REMEMBER (and a sequel) was also adapted for screen by Crown Media and multiple other titles by Melissa are currently in development for film and TV.

Visit her website at
www.melissahill.info
Or get in touch via social media.

f [Instagram]

Printed in Great Britain
by Amazon

54325010R00079